UBOA ACT 1

UBOA ACT 1

Prince Otchere

This book is dedicated to my late father Peter, my
mother Leticia, my wife Cheri, my children Prince,
Malaika and Cameron. Also, to my family, friends and
close supporters. Thank you.
"We Give God the Glory."

Contents

1

The Father and Son

In the beginning God created man and called the creature "Son" and in return "Son" regarded God as his creator and father. "Son" was a strange little creature hairless and helpless with plumped toes, and tiny little fingers which were balled into small fists. The creature's tiny body and small frame allowed the creature to be nestled comfortably between the king's bosoms and arm. God relished over his new creation discovering within the fragile creature of man a new sense of pride and purpose.

God was very much excited at having become the founder and sole proprietor of a grand and noble being. Instilled within "Son" harbored all the hopes and dreams of his father and creator. God had never crafted a creature more sublime and mesmerizing as the creature "Son". The creature was uniquely tailored and flawless in makeup and design. The conception and creation of man would forever serve as a testimonial to the king's mastery and skill. "You will grow", the king announced," to change this world for within you all things are possible." The frail infant offered his master and creator a rejuvenated sense of purpose as ruler and king. God was a remarkable physicist very much skilled in the art of alchemy and amalgamation. The king rejoiced on this day at having completed and finished his greatest opus and body of work.

God was enamored with joy and filled with disbelief behind the success of his conquest and the range of his artistry. He marveled over the small infant sized being consumed with bewildering fascination and astonishment. An impish grin began to form across the king's face peering down looking directly into the eyes of his latest creation. God recalled the toil and extent to which he labored and worked to ensure "Son's" vitality and homeostasis working tirelessly to bestow within the spirit of the creature the breath of new life. Though the creature's initial gestation and development was daunting and time-consuming God found himself becoming infatuated and utterly engrossed over his new obsession.

At the time only the thought of perfection engulfed and occupied the king's mind. Every nip, and every tuck, every mold and fold measured precisely as to avoid errors. "Son's" fingers and toes were perfectly proportioned and exact in likeness and though the task was challenging the creators hard work and efforts finally paid off. His greatest achievement had now been fully conceptualized and brought to fruition. The king was unabashed and held no reservations in viewing Son as a masterpiece. The creature was flawlessly designed and masterfully crafted, very much so that the king could not help but be impressed at his own conjuring.

It was a most happy and joyful occasion for the great king who had experienced several unsuccessful and misfortunate attempts before this moment of success. "Son" was unlike any creature or being God had ever fashioned before. The creature was incomparably different having been sculpted and designed entirely in the image and likeness of his himself. God had finally achieved success in producing the perfect specimen to help assist in accomplishing his most grand, and illustrious plan.

This celebratory occasion reflected Gods will and crowning achievement in crafting the perfect prototype of its kind. God was successful in his prospective ambition to secure the perfect creature to help assist him in completing his grand and masterful plan. Son was the last cog and the final missing piece that would ultimately push and propel Gods plans into motion. Man's existence would be necessary if not essential to God in fulfilling his glorious and somewhat lofty goal of supreme domination over the celestial realms and universe. The only dilemma presently facing the king was that the fragile creation "Son" was not fully formed and would require several decades of incubation before the creature would be ready to accept his ordained position of power.

Nevertheless, the king still rejoiced glowing with exuberance and pride. God was without a doubt a happy and delighted ruler, "I am finally done," smiled the king, marveling over his latest creation. "You will grow to become a great earthly keeper reigning in my absence and maintain order here. You will aspire to create, and design like I, and help this beautiful land to flourish and grow and eventually decorate the entire world." God cradled the infant in his arms, and together they walked. "Son" would become Gods last and final creation inside of Eden.

2

The Eden

Eden at the time was a vast botanical garden that housed all of God's many creations. It was the heart and very epicenter in which all creatures dwelled and resided. Eden served as the capital for the newly developed supercontinent and world called earth. The Pangea at the time though enormous and vast was ignored and undeveloped except for the garden of Eden. The garden of Eden housed a metropolis of exotic creatures and wildlife that accounted for its massive population. The astonishing number of creatures that lived in Eden ranged in rarity and were each unique in their design. The utopian land of Eden was a paradise like none had ever seen. Not a single imagination could fathom the splendor and beauty of the flourishing vast land. The rich fertile soil provided a luxurious landscape of tall grass which pastured over the land like thin bristles. The thin blades of green grass covered the surface of Eden stretching out for miles like plush carpeting.

Each morning the sun would appear to greet the land shining its rays over Eden. The sun's radiance and warmth extended outward like warm arms stretching beyond the horizon. Eden was also home to the most rearrest and delicate of flowers, these blooming plants help to decorate the garden splendidly. The quiet serenity and peaceful wind land allowed for both pollen and blossom petals to languish aimlessly amongst the monarchs and other delicate butterflies. The fertile land was ripe and blossomed abundantly with produce and vegetation. The bushes and trees offered tasty fruits and berries for the inhabitants of Eden. Not creature in Eden went hungry nor were they neglected or denied access to basic needs essential for their survival. The provisional needs of the Eden were met and sustained through an intricate network and ecosystem. The creatures thrived and flourished interdependently with each member living and working in the spirit of community to maintain the dignity and standard of their dwelling. The earthly oasis Eden flourished abundantly thriving with vigor and life, it was a wonderland that shimmered with innocence and gleamed with endless possibilities.

In all the vastness of the world, Eden was but a simple pin, placed in the center of a large and barren wasteland we know now to be earth. And despite not being extraordinary in size, Eden was very much a kept and homely place. The garden was an ideal paradise that served as a functional habitat which help to support a vast number of species all living peacefully in cohabitation. At the time there existed in Eden an assortment and variation of colorful creatures. There lived in Eden, creatures with short tails, and some with lengthy ones. Some creatures owned long noses, beaks, and snouts, while some others were snub and short. Some creatures were draped with fur, while others, robed in leather and feathers. The many rivers of Eden help to accommodate a catalogue of aquatic creatures, the waters served as home to the many crustaceous and scaly creatures many of their neighbors possessing gills and fins as well. On land there were creatures that walked on four legs, and some that were fortunate and did not walk at all, but instead soared unreserved through the sky with only the wind beneath their wings. Every creature was miraculous in their design and was brought forth to life by the king himself. This extensive collection of creature's man would eventually come to categorize and classify as animals. Eden was a land of peace and tranquility with all its inhabitants existing collaboratively in perfect harmony and unisons. The residents honored an unspoken code and conduct of civil decency and mutual respect. In the plentiful land of Eden there was no need to hog or horde, because the generous land was bountiful and for a long time this is how life went on in the beautiful paradise.

3

The Creatures

God was an artist, the earth was his canvas, and with a stroke of love, he brought creatures to life. God became the king, protector and ultimately the provider for his creatures. The provisional qualities exemplified by God are what held together his celestial title as "father of all things and the renowned creator of all life". However, unlike his other creations the rearing and caring of the new creature "Son" would require a great deal of time and attention from the king.

From the moment the sun shone; peeking its rays to welcome the day, God could be found in the presence and company of the new creature. He reared and nursed over his creation and naturally as time passed, so would their bond. The two became inseparable; sharing a pure and innocent love that could only exist between a child, and its creator. "Love" God explained to the infant creature, "is what keeps you alive, it is the direct source of your strength and power." Staring at "Son" in fascination and bewildering amusement. The king thought to himself "I have finally done it." God revealed, feeling somewhat accomplished, "I have created the perfect creature to harness, and store my spiritual energy and life source."

"Son" was the first creature to be categorized and classified as man. The creatures of the garden owned their own identities, and classifications in respects to their breed, however man was a uniquely different type of species. Man was the first creature engineered to be autonomous and self-governing. A creature able to source and store the potential energy of love. "Son" possessed the capability to distill and refine hatred and negativity into purest form of energy, love.

Love was at the time a rare commodity which could neither be bought nor sold. The raw energy could only be produced through the service of gratitude and generosity. It served to benefit the king to create creatures that could hold and store such profound energy. Man reserved the ability to absorb negative energy by removing the adverse impurities by way of refinement. This cleansing process allowed for God to safely stiffen and draw energy from the love and admiration of its host.

The creature man contained within its body and mind the conscious ability to discern between right and wrong. These insightful powers were restricted and commonly reserved for the highest beings and lifeforms. God was amused by his grand accomplishment in having finally created the perfect creature to help further his ambitions.

It was commonly understood at the time that God's drew his strength from the love he received from his creations and subjects. The finite precious material eventually became the essence and fabric of God's being, as the raw energy was known to strengthen and enhance the kings' powers substantially. Love was to God, what food and water was to man or any creatures under his domain. Affection and respect were highly prized resources essential for a king, or any leader determined to keep themselves enthroned in power.

It was believed that a king or ruler who receives unconditional love from their subjects could rule for as long that love sustains. This notion provided understanding as to why God sought desperately after the rare and somewhat vital energy. The procurement of such celestial energy would ultimately assure God's sustainability and eternal reign over heaven and earth. God had at the time only one concern that occupied his thoughts and irritated his mind. It was the fear of someday exhausting this natural and most precious of resources. The anxiety and concern of possibly losing his throne and power to a less than competent successor.

This uncontainable fear only helped to serve the king's insatiable need to gather, store and even hoard the special energy. The containment of love is what ultimately fueled the king's motive and desire to form and create such an assortment of strange and rather unique creatures. Each creature was responsible in doing their part to assure the production of the vital energy. The king's fixation with love prompted him to forge matter and create the planet earth. The planet served as an enormous warehouse was designed with the sole purpose of gathering and storing potentiated energy.

At the time earth was an underdeveloped planet, however it contained the perfect conditions to efficiently manufacture the vital energy resource. What began as a recreational hobby eventually developed into a skill and trade for the king. In his early experiments while still a novice God preoccupied his time conjuring mostly insects and rodents before moving on to craft larger species of mammals and other creatures. The inhabitants of Eden at the time were God's most valued creations and subjects. He took pride in feeding, grazing and leading his creations like a shepherd watching carefully over his flock. All while harnessing the vital energy produced by his creations. The creatures unyielding admiration and appreciation for God would be necessary to feed and sustain the insatiable hunger and ego of an omnipotent and powerful king. The only concern or issue the king faced was that the creatures could only produce a limited number of the precious energy in small increments and doses. God attempted to replicate and forge different variations of species yet none of these creatures could conduct or distill the necessary energy which at the time equated to only a fraction of the love and energy that he received from his gathering of heavenly subjects and followers in heaven, until now.

The king held the creature "Son" in his arms and could feel the glow of energy and love pulsating around the child's body. God could feel the soothing sensation of warmth radiating through him and sensing his strength and power increasing gradually. God recognized the profound energy being garnered by the small creature "Son" was processing and amplifying the love and affection being demonstrated by the king. "Son" was successful in returning to his father and creator the vital life-force in its most purists and potent form. God relished the thought of experiencing the full energy and potential of "Son" and appeared somewhat pleased at the thought of multiplying his strength and advancing his position. At present the small creature "Son" was only capable of producing a small amount of energy in proportion to its current size and strength. The king smiled to himself as if amused by the amount of potential energy that could be sourced once "Son" has been fully formed and completed the final stage of maturation.

4

The Visit

High above Eden in the realms of heaven trouble began to brew. The kingdom held a vacant throne, that was seldom occupied by the divine king. It was believed that God, was devoting too much of his time, and energy on earth. The citizens castigated the king for his absence chastising him for spending all his time with his earthly projects. The king was accused of neglecting his other, more important duties such as presiding as the sovereign and reigning ruler over the heavenly world.

One day an unannounced guest appeared in the garden. An angel arrived on earth to deliver an important message for the king. The angel brought with him word of mutiny, and treachery forming within the kingdom. The angel appeared suddenly before his master and king, who at the time was in the middle of tending to his new creature. God developed a casual routine of caring for the creature "Son." often enjoying their frequent visits to the hot springs where he bathed the creature in clear warm water. However, this time the tender moment was rudely disrupted by the familial spirit and presence of their uninvited guest. "Your highness," interrupted the angel, "I do not mean to hinder this tender moment, but I must inform you of something wicked and foul unfolding in the midst of your kingdom."

God appeared unbothered and did not budge, shake or tremble at the angel's announcement. He instead continued to focus his attention on the present task of bathing his child. The angel began to grow annoyed and upset by the lack of concern displayed by the king in response to his warnings. The passive dismissal and insult would not be enough to detour the misguided angel from furthering the purpose of his quest. The angel was determined to express and share his report and unload a host of troubling information and news.

"Your highness, the elders, and high courts are beginning to question the welfare of your sanity, some believe that you are ill at mind. You spend all your time here on earth watching over these fragile creatures, more less mortal beings." The troubled angel peered suspiciously, studying over the strange hairless creature seeming rather repulsed and unimpressed. "It is as if you no longer regard the heavens as your sanctuary and home. This unscheduled sabbatical only helps to reaffirm the notion that you seek to escape from the kingdom and resign your celestial reign."

Drawing a long slow glare, the angel searched desperately for an indication of fear on the face and brows of his king but found God unfazed. The angel continued with his reprieve fully aware that his intrusive arrival cast a gloomy cloud over what was to be a peaceful and intimate moment. The angel's provocation and ill intentions becoming somewhat apparent by his behavior that he would not be satisfied until he received a response to his malingering threats.

"They all speculate," he continued uninterrupted, "that you have been seated on your throne for much too long, very much so that the taste of power has finally intoxicated you. You no longer seem concerned with the needs and wellbeing of your citizens or subjects." The angels voice slithered with accusations as he spoke, "Tell me have you become lamed, or simply grown indifferent to the matters and concerns in which I have brought to your attention?" God did not respond, his attention very much distracted consumed mostly by the sounds of coos and gargling noises being produced by the small creature fastened on his shoulder.

"I might be inclined to agree with the rebellion above," The angel patronized openly understanding fully that his crass like behavior had longed breached the boundaries of his proper rank and station. Any intelligent angel if given the option would rather cut out and remove their tongue before choosing to speak out publicly against the king. This manner of disrespect and insubordination was unheard of by the king, never having witnessed or experienced such a high degree of contempt than at this very moment. "Tell me then," the angel continued, "is it true that you are you not well, and presently ill at the mind? I personally dismissed such falsehoods and regard such idle talk as untrue. However, considering today's interaction I beg to agree." The remark drew a sudden halt evoking silent tension between the two figures. The kettling air surrounding them seem to whistle with intensity but still nothing happened. God's inaction and silence served as encouragement enough for the syndicate to continue behaving menacingly. The angel gave a disagreeing shake of his head and sucked his teeth in expressing his disappointment. The display of disrespect was unsettling and seem to demonstrate a blatant disregard of the king's superiority over him. In bearing witness to such an encounter, anyone looking on would be correct draw confusion at the questionable dynamic of their relationship.

God remained civil but was by no means inattentive to the interest of the unwelcoming and somewhat irritating visitor. Listening on silently, God offered little acknowledgment to the intrusive visitor. Though he did not feel compelled to react he was keenly perceptive observing every word being spewed by the mischievous angel. The nuisance of allegations and passive threats made by the rambunctious angel in his ramblings did not fall short of the king's ears, but not well enough to detour God from completing his routine.

God bathed the creature at the same time every morning. The moment was intended to be peaceful and serene, however today the task fared somewhat awkward and impersonal with the prying eyes of their inhospitable guest. God inhaled a heaping gust of air, and deliberately blew it over the small child. The sudden gust caused the child to coo and laugh out playfully. The small infantile creature appeared to enjoy the tender moment just as much if not more than his mentor and creator. God was protective of the creature treating the delicate child with profound care and tenderness. He regarded the occupation as being no different from that of a gardener desiring nothing more than to produce an outstanding yield or wanting to grow a rare and unique flower the first of its kind.

"Must you waste all your time with this horrid creature!" intruded the angel, growing rather impatient. The stinging remark was seen as an insult aimed to deface the king's very creation of which God attributed to as his greatest masterpiece. God was now visibly upset with his visitor and wanted nothing more than to remove the mischievous angel from existence. The angel was now smirking pridefully after having accomplished his initial goal of irritating and annoying the king. He was all but unaware the wrath and fury upon which God was preparing to unleash over the ill-mannered guest.

Loud thunder began to erupt violently from the sky and just as the king was about to unfurl his onslaught of his wrath over the contemptuous angel, "achoo" sneezed the young prince. The soft sound landed gently on the ears of the heavenly father drawing his attention from the contentious angel back to caring for his creation. God looked down at the creatures face only to find himself immediately disarmed and drawn by the adorable look of innocence. "Son" served as a wonderful distraction for the king who found himself staring down into the big round eyes looking helplessly up at him. The creatures gleamed and shimmered like a glowing orb reflecting his own image. In viewing himself through the reflective lenses of the small infant God quickly collected his composure feeling somewhat embarrassed by his behavior. In that instance God was reminded of his violent temper and was able to quickly detach from the negative frequency of emotions stirring within him. The thick fog of clouds covering the sky began to suddenly lift and disperse. God did not want to upset or startle the tender creature understanding that exposure to frightening and violent scenes could cause unnecessary trauma and stagnation for his creation.

The king decided it best to continue ignoring the angel, in hopes the visitor would pick up on the inaudible cue that his unwarranted intrusion was unwelcome. The anguished angel did not flee, nor would he retreat despite the observable neglect and treatment. The impatient angle was all but unaware the courtesy and grace being currently being afforded to him by the patience and generosity of the king. The angel in response to being openly ignored, felt as though his words were falling on deaf ears and was prepared if not persistent in carrying on and continuing his defaming speech. However just as he was preparing to speak, the angel stopped finding himself confused and distracted by the strange behavior being displayed by the king.

"I suppose you are right son," God declared suddenly, responding to the indistinguishable chatter and gurgling of his small creation. "Silence will not discourage our visitors departure, and it seems that ignoring him will not work either." Waving his finger playfully over the child, God asked, "what shall we do?" the creature smiled and answered with loud cry of laughter. Suddenly a thought struck the king. God began to grin as he concocted a grand idea that was sure to rid them of the pesky angel. The grin began to grow and form a large smile plastered across his face. He intended to demonstrate his disinterest and indifference to the angel presence.

"Ha, ha, hah!" God cried out repeatably expelling bellowing heaps of laughter. He purposefully splashed water over the creature's face which instantly provoked the child to join in with laughter and excitement. The act was a familiar form of play between the pair that occurred during their routine bathing rituals, God knew that splashing water over the creature would provoke laughter from the small creature. And though unscripted with no time to rehearse the tiny creature performed marvelously. The small creature reacted excitably and began shouting, cooing, and laughing uncontrollably. Together, father and son celebrated in an animated uproar of celebration and laughter, the occasion was truly a delightful spectacle to view.

The intimate display between father and son would have been enough to ward, away any individual, or persons not wanting to disturb or impose on such a tender moment. But our visitor was neither amused, nor touched by the closeness of their bond, but instead found his king's behavior deplorable feeling completely repulsed by the intimate display. The tiny creature gave out another wave of laughter, and this made God smile. He followed behind the child's accompanying the loud shrieking sound with bellowing laughter of his own. "Ha, ha, ha, ha!" laughed God, finally turning to acknowledge and address the seemingly nonexistent angel occupying space around them. "It seems that your silly nonsensical ramblings indeed serve a great purpose here. You have managed to successfully join the ranks of a lowly court jester. Your foolish actions today have only help to confirm that you are and have always been a pitiful clown suited solely for the purpose of entertainment. And though I confess I am neither moved nor amused by your antics. However, it seems that your absurd behavior brings great amusement and joy to my small creature."

God stretched forth his arm to present the creature like a celebratory trophy, "Just listen to how he laughs at you." God kept his poise playfully splashing the child from soothing warm waters and holding him close to his body. The innocently happy creature was all but unaware of the growing tension forming between God and the unnamed visitor behaving as most infants and began to mutter and laugh out loud. "Son" shrieked uncontrollably carrying on louder than before. The jovial sound of play and laughter seem to upset and irritate the annoyed angel. More offensive was the deliberate exposition of the creature naked body and bottom being paraded about. The angel was tempted to react and speak out against at the incorrigible child, but before he could speak out the startling voice of his master gripped him before he could utter a sound or make a statement.

"Do you want to know why I created this creature?" God proposed, but strangely the talkative angel did not speak or attempt to answer. The angel seemed vexed but held his composure and waited for his master to explain. "It is odd that you have no words" God teased, "when just moments ago you were so candor in your proclamations." The king paused a moment to allow the angel another opportunity to respond. However, the precarious angel did not answer but retreated quietly recalling his proper rank and place. "It appears that you and the many others have forgotten the power of my voice." God animated slowly moving away from the streaming water floating delicately over the grassy knolls. "I have not lost my senses; in fact, I see clearly what must be done." Looking over at the creature in his arm, "I have created this creature to become my sole heir, the one to inherit my kingdom. He will become king, my successor and ruler of both heaven and earth."

The bewildered angel looked surprisingly shocked and stunned with confusion. "k'-k-king" he stammered to complete the word. "Yes,' reassured God "when the time comes, I will promote this creature elevating him to the ranks of godliness." God unveiled his masterful plan revealing as to the reason for his extended absences. It became apparent to the angel that the king had gone quite senile and was outright disposed of his wits. "And so, this is this how you have been occupying your time," declared the angel who by now had recovered his nerves and began to speak belligerently. "Squandering precious time coordinating your own resignation and retirement."

"I simply refuse to keep a kingdom," answered God, shooting a fierce gaze in the direction of the rancid angel that froze his nerves and sent a cold chill down his spine. "Wherever treachery and treason run ramped and unchecked," Turning his attention back over to the small creature who was now dry and nestled safely in his father's arm. The angel looked queerly over at the child, his eyes searching for something amazing or strangely unique about the creature but found nothing distinctive or special in the creature's makeup or physical characteristics. The angel who's first impression of the infant drew utter repulsion was now coupled with embittered prejudice viewing the small creature as a threat to celestial status quo. The angel regarded the infantile creature as a blemished attempt to replace and remove the current faculty of his heavenly cabinet. God's creation was not well received and appeared to angel as being a botched replica of a wingless angle. The creature appeared as an affront to God's legion of angels and loyal followers. "Your highness," interjected the angel, no longer able to contain his thoughts or remain silent any longer. "Why would you offer to bestow the throne of both heaven, and earth onto a creature such as this…this…" The pressured angel appeared to struggle in his speech considering his next choice of words carefully, "mortal!" The disappointing words spat out from his mouth, seeming slightly irritated, and wrought with offense because he, himself was overlooked and not considered to fill the dutiful position and role.

"Why not give your throne to one of your other children, the ones that dwell in your kingdom. Your children who passionately love and adore you, there are so many who have longed for such an opportunity." The angel could no longer conceal his selfish motives revealing his longing thirst for power that was becoming more apparent in his speech. He reeked of a foul insatiable odor the very scent and aroma of vile corruption and wickedness that resonated seeping from his pores. "Do we not deserve it more," questioned the embittered angel in a fierce and harsh tone. However, God did would not answer or offer a response, "Are we not your loyal subjects…" cried the angel, "…worthy of your love and admiration." God was done talking and concluded the engagement drawing closer in the path of his visitor, who seemed to involuntarily move out of the way to allow for his master pass, and yet still close enough to hear the scornful reply of his master in passing. "No, those children do not."

The angel appeared somewhat satisfied and happy to have received such a harsh and direct response from the king. It seems the clever angel had gotten exactly what he had come down to secure; objectionable truth the inadmissible confirmation that their king and ruler was unfit. The angel rejoiced with a snarling laugh and begged the king once more for assurance, "please, tell me again." he taunted loudly, "you mustn't be coy now, say it once more so that the universe can hear you this time." Turning his ears to his king, the angel shut his eyes as though to playfully heighten his senses. "Please do not revoke your thoughts," the angel teased on, "repeat your words." The angel had barely opened his eyes before finding himself face to face in the grips of his master's glare. The shock of God's sudden appearance frightened the angel who quickly jumped back in surprise stumbling backwards onto the floor. The king stood over the cowering angel, towering dramatically over the fallen creature, "no, my children do not…" God repeated fearlessly "…deserve to bear the weight and grunt of my troubles on their shoulders."

"So, you love us that much," responded the angel sarcastically, "that you refuse to turn over the kingdom to us." The angel growing superficially amused began to laugh out insidiously, "If you really expect myself, of any of the high Supremes to believe or accept any part of this blatant scandal, then my lord I really do question the sake of your sanity." The angel offered his insults from what he believed to be a safe range and distance. But suddenly, God was upon the angel again, closer in proximity than before. "Do you enjoy doing that?" asked God stoically, "Is that your only trick," The angel, tried to utter a response but could not any audible sounds and was in a sense at a loss for words. The kings boiling temper resembled that of a volcano churning ready to explode at any moment. But unlike that of an erupting volcano the king was able to defuse his temper from becoming explosive, especially with the creature son, lodged in his arm.

"Your trickery will not work with me, as it does so well with the others." God declared triumphantly "I refuse to allow the seeds of deception to flourish and thrive within the confines my kingdom. God looked squarely into the eyes of the angel, who found himself shaken up by the intensity and fierceness of the king's gaze. "Tell me then, who deserves of my throne?" The angel stammered backwards attempting to walk away but found himself ensnared and pinned between his massive ego, and the furious wrath of his anguished king. "Do you believe yourself more capable than I?" asked God, "as if you, yourself are immune to the temptation and allure of sin. It became apparent to God that envy and pride had consumed the treacherous angel, and possibly penetrated his kingdom and fortress infecting his subjects and others.

The king laughed loudly at the angel scoffing at the idea that he would consider ever allowing such a wretched creature or any angel to reign over the heavenly empire of his kingdom. "You angel's must really take me for a mad fool, a king without his wits." God, leaned in closer to the quivering angel, "tell the elders," He whispered looking directly into the face of the nervous angel, "not to worry themselves on the subject and matter of my mental health and wellness. I decide and do as I choose fit answering to no one. I would rather raise and anoint a full-bred mortal, than promote that of an underserving demigod to take my place." "Son" was still being cradled in between God arms tucked safely and securely at the king's side. "You will all see, when the time is right this creature will become the ruler of both, man, and angels alike." God stepped aside releasing the somewhat caged bird allowing for unobstructed path of egress for the frightened angel to take his leave.

The Angel was a bit distressed by the news he just received, and looking at the child inches before him. The angel did not want to be ruled by the likes of a mortal being especially that of an inferior and creedless race. "Go now!" shouted God, "and report your findings to the council. Notify the kingdom of my decision exactly as I have described them to you. I shall be returning home very soon to verify my intentions before the Supreme council and ministry."

The cue to take leave was indicated by a gesturing wave of the king's hand. The angel quickly unfastened his wings, and just as he was about to make his departure, he found himself stuck; snagged by the heavy binding chain his kings' final message, "where there is chaos, I shall restore order." The king fell silent, but the angel did not move, he seemed rather troubled by the idea and threat of restoration. "Go now!" God demanded with disdain in his tone, "flee from my sight as I command it." The angel managed to free himself from the trance like state after being engrossed in deep thought. The angel without sparing another word did as his master ordered and quickly left Eden to return to the heavens. The angel's pride was bruised but not broken and as he soared into the air so did his thoughts imagining the many ways, he would enact vengeance and redeem his shattered confidence and bruised ego.

5

The Prelude

God had already foreseen the impeding crises approaching and considered numerous resolutions and ways in which to remedy the situation. Still tempered and irritated by the intrusion of the unwanted guest, the king managed to retain his humility by containing his calm and poised like demeanor. His primary concern at the time was in ensuring and safety and preservation the life of his beloved creation. God contemplating several resolutions, considered the notion of bringing the creature "Son" into the heavenly realms with him but dismissed the idea considering the distant voyage as being far too dangerous and turbulent to embark. The creature was much too small, and frail to accompany God on the long journey. And even if the creature managed to make it through to the celestial kingdom, "Son" would be much too vulnerable to be left alone. "Those jealous angels," thought God, "would do anything to foil my plans, including destroying my creation." Suddenly, the king was struck with a profound thought and idea.

"Yes," God smiled openly, "I know what I must do." he declared "I must find the creature son a suitable guardian for the meantime, someone to protect, and care for my creation until my timely return." "But who?" God stopped to consider all his creatures and selected only the finest candidates suitable for the dutiful assignment, He weighed heavily over the distinctive attributes and qualities of each creature. It took God some time before coming to the decision of who he would choose to foster and guard his creation during his absence. "Tree!" he echoed to himself, "Yes. Tree is perfect. She is the most suited of my creations to assign the governing role." Quickly, the king gathered his thoughts, and slung the child across his shoulder, and began to move forward in the direction of the royal forest.

God presumed that the traitorous angel had already reached the realms of heaven by now. Time was quickly becoming an elusive instrument that seem to taunt the king causing him great anguish and strife. Despite his growing worries God, would not hasten his stride moving ever so delicately through the forest. Traveling with his small companion placed comfortably over his heart and chest. As he walked, the king was overcome with an overwhelming sense of sadness. God grieved over the thought of being separated from his beloved creation. He damned the treacherous angel and cursed the heavens above for having disrupted his solace and state of peace. The king knew that it would be a long time before he would be able to hold and embrace his tender creation again.

"I wish I could be here to watch you grow, transforming from a child into a man, like a prince into a king. Your ascent will be astonishing." The moment was sad, the creature began to weep, as if it too could sense the melancholy atmosphere that dampened the air. "Do not cry my child," said God, attempting to pacify the creature with soothing words, I will be absent from your life, but I will always keep watch over you." "Do you understand?" but the creature did not stop crying. The loud cries echoed loudly through the royal forest. The pouring outcry was a strange and foreign sound that startled the nearby creatures and animals looking on. "Do not cry" God attempted to reassure his child again, "I will return to bring you home with me, and together we will reign over the heavens." God pacified his creation with a coddling smile. The small child grew silently agreeable. "Much better," affirmed the king with growing sense of relief, "Do you want to know why I have chosen Tree, to foster and care for you?" God monodical engagement appeared to have a soothing affect over the small and tender child. The two walked on together distracted in heavy discussion as they entered the heart of the Eden into the royal forest to meet with Tree.

6

The Grand Tree

God appeared to Tree, "Hello, my good friend," he walked towards her; Tree quickly recognized the boisterous voice of her immaculate king. He moved with ease and grace, and a gentleness in his stride. God seem to glide delicately across the land advancing gracefully in her the direction carried forth by the subtle soft winds. He passed gently nearly motionless, his feet barley grazing the grassy earth. Tree was unsure as to the reason or purpose for her king's unwarranted and impromptu visit. It was a striking surprise for Tree to see the king without receiving notice beforehand. Usually, God's visits would be announced and celebrated throughout Eden prior to his arrival. The image of God walking thru the garden, as though an ordinary being was a truly priceless sight to behold. Tree's attention quickly shifted after taking notice to the strange little creature tucked in between her lordship's arms.

"Greetings, your highness," Tree announced, respectfully offering her king a radiating smile in place a meaning handshake. God received the warm smile and proceeded to exchange pleasantries with Tree. "Salutations my dearest and eldest friend". Tree, seemed mesmerized by her king's presence, somewhat in disbelief at his sudden and unannounced appearance, "It is a pleasure to see you out and about, and looking well my sire."

"Thank you, Tree, my friend. I am well, but the question of my health is neither the subject nor the reason for my visit today." Tree

25

could sense concern in the king's voice. "I come to you today, to ask for your help." "My help," replied Tree, "but, your highness, I am but a simple tree, what could I possibly do for anyone, especially for a king. God laughed at Tree's remarks, "Tree, my friend, there is no other creature to whom I would entrust to fulfill this most humbling request." God moved closer to Tree and placed his palm against her body. "Tree you are as wise as time and are as noble as you are benevolent. Nowhere else in this garden could I find a truer friend. Just look how well you have managed to transform this small plot of land into a thriving garden and forest. I am forever indebted owing to you all the beauty and splendor the surrounds Eden. You have helped Eden to flourish wonderfully and decked the garden quite elegantly."

Tree quickly realized that her lordships flattery was not in vain. She knew the king better than anyone else. Tree knew the royal compliments being paid to her would un-doughtily cost her later down the line concluding most likely with a taxing request disguised as a favor. Tree listened patiently as the king continued, "Tree I need your help nursing, and rearing my most recent creation." God stretched out his arms outward, so that Tree could see up close the small infant child in full view. Tree was speechless, surprisingly shocked by the strange request, however uncertain as to how react or respond. She stood stunned searching her cluttered mind for a permeable thought but gathered no plausible response to the request. But before Tree could utter a word or response, the king continued his plea.

"I am sorry," God apologized "to have to thrust on to you this huge burden and responsibility. But I gravely need your assistance." "Tree," God paused in a dramatic fashion, "there is treachery and mutiny within my kingdom above. I fear that great misfortunes in heaven are unbraiding as we speak. I can no longer trust the intentions of my jealous subjects and angels. Heaven is no longer a safe sanctuary but has become a paradise lost. I must return to heaven to restore order amidst the chaos of the storm. I plan to expose and condemn the treasonous traitor and expel those involved before hurling them into the abysmal pits."

Tree, listened on with widened ears, and sadden eyes, "I cannot return home with the creature," the king continued, "as I can foresee the contemptuous regard of those jealous angels, consumed with fear and hatred they will conspire and plot to rid the innocent creature of its life." The king paused a moment, staring far off and beyond, "But I cannot," he regained his thoughts, "let them defile my greatest creation. Those angels are right to fear this new creature man and cannot begin to fathom the creatures' boundless and limitless powers." God turned his gaze back onto Tree, "And so I plea to you Tree," he concluded "aide me, to protect, and sustain, this new creation, so that he may grow safely to ascend to his rightful place and fulfill his destiny. I have quickly come to cherish this creature and believe that you will grow to love him as well. Take good care my child and take special notice to the size of his heart for as his love grows so will his form and body begin to take shape." The king concluded his request not before adding "Unfortunately, I do not know when I will be back for my creation, but have faith that when the time is right, I shall return to secure and retrieve my subject and shall reward you wonderfully."

Tree listened to her master's words with a growing dislike for direction of their conversation. "Your Highness" She quickly interrupted, "why place the child with me? You have designed, so many other creatures, with amazing details and abilities. You have molded many fantastic creatures that are suited to rear a child, why place the guardianship of such a delicate creature into my clumsy hands and possession." Looking over at her bough limbs, and extended branches "or better yet, my lack of hands to be more precise." Tree was right, that in the Eden there were plenty of creatures that were more suitable, in assuring the safety of this new creature than she, but God simply laughed at her testimonial, and reassured Tree, "Do not worry my good friend for Eden will be under my special protection. After my departure today, no one will be permitted or able to enter Eden."

Tree grew flustered, and frustrated that her king was not being sympathetic to her plea, "As you are my lord," she answered, "as you command it, I shall obey, but not before expressing my discerning discontent to the proposed idea." Tree looked at her king with annoyance. "I am merely a tree, a simple tree!" she repeated, "I have seen other creatures, nurse and rear their offspring, and witnessed for myself the overwhelming pressures and stressors of child rearing. It is quite an ordeal and shaming sight. I will be unable to keep the poor creature from wandering aimlessly nor can I give chase and run after him when necessary to provide the infant protection from impeding dangers. What if I the creature disobeys me and ignores my many warnings and somehow wanders deep into the trenches of lion's territory. A small creature such as this in the company those hungry lions would not fare well..."

Tree quickly paused her words looking into the face of her master finding him exceptionally unamused by her reasoning. She instantly ended her dramatic and playful conclusion, which could easily be mistaken, and misinterpreted as a passive covert form of treason which could be insinuated as being a sly or idling threat. With a pretentious smile, and a quick slight of tongue Tree wit-fully shifted the conversation away from the rubbish idea of hungry lions.

"Your highness, I mean no disrespect, I am clumsy in my effort to convey my physical limitations. I am deeply rooted and thus cannot guarantee the safety of your child in my care. To leave such a delicate creature with me is a most unfortunate idea, if I may suggest, if it makes no difference that you consider placing the child atop the highest mountain." God drew a grim face, displaying his discontent. This time Tree could not catch her tongue fast enough and resolved to salvage her blundering words with a questionable plea, "I, mean no disrepute, my king, the tallest mountain top would definitely ensure that the two of you would always remain close, and near one another." But it was much too late. Tree could not repair the damage caused by her unfiltered words nor could she mend them with more falsehoods.

Alas, she gave out an exhausting sigh, waiting patiently to receive the repercussions for her insubordinate conduct and behavior. Tree did not know what punitive measures to expect and drew her eyes shut. She prepared to embrace her king's, wrath awaiting a scorning reprimand for her conduct and display of contempt. Tree nervousness was apparent as she struggled to pry open her shuttering eyes.

Tree stood before the king with squinted eyes as though facing the sun in all its radiance. She resembled a child when caught in the act of foul play, expecting a fierce scolding. Surprisingly, God, did not strike her down, or smite her with foul harsh insults instead he laughed out loud, and, laughed again. The contagious laughter continued to grow and soon infected Tree, as she nervously joined in on the laughter. The king was amused by Tree's sense of wit and good humor. Their laughter slowly settled, "Tree!" answered God, "I have not laughed like this in many centuries, you're truly as humorous, as you're fun. And though you jest in good faith, my dear friend, my heart does not desire amusement. No, not while evil lurks infectiously contaminating my kingdom."

God paused for a moment at the thought of his dwindling kingdom, then shook away the idea, and continued, "Tree, I have chosen you because you are my first original creation, and without you nothing here in Eden would exist. It is no secret that you have done exceedingly well. I gave to you the gift of life, and in return you have given me a bountiful scenery of green pastures. The paradise Eden is largely indebted to you with its inhabitants having nothing but admiration and respect for you. You will have at your disposal the entire kingdom, and all its creatures, to help aid you in the rearing of the young creature. You have taken charge of this garden to make it into a paradise. I am confident that you will not disappoint me and do as you see fit in my absence." God gently Placed the child gently onto the high flattops of Tree's soft bushy treetop making for a suitable pen to house and hold the new creature. God prepared for his departure, but not before reassuring Tree, "Listen, you must believe that I would never give you more than you can handle. Goodbye my dear friend Tree, until we meet again." then instantly, the king was gone vanishing instantly.

The king's hasty departure and un-timely exit help only to infuriate Tree, who still had questions, and reprieves to be answered, however it was too late, God was gone. The sun was now beginning to set, the dimming sky slowly clearing to make room for the moon and stars to make their appearance and illuminate the sky. The wind blew gently evoking an air a peace and tranquility over the land. The new creature laid, peacefully asleep Tree's leafy head. Tree was tempted to bring the creature down to take a closer look. But discovered that she was much too tired and exhausted by the ordeal of today's dealings. Tree decided it best to follow the example set by the new prince, and get some sleep, and hopefully in the morning she would be well rested for the long day ahead.

7

The Winged Messenger

In the morning Tree called out to her closest companions Heron, and Crane. The birds heard Tree's call and quickly flew down to greet her. Heron, and Crane were Tree's winged friends and trusted companions. The two friends ventured about the various areas of Eden, flying, and traveling freely about viewing at great distance the furthest unknown regions of the garden. The adventurous pair were well versed in arial exploration with decades of flying experience surveying the vast parameters of the garden. They crossed over rivers, and trenching lakes, soaring high above the tropical waterfalls and mountain peaks. Their feathery wings visiting parts and regions of Eden that have never been viewed or explored by other creatures. They often returned home from their adventures bearing wonderful stories of strange, and unbelievable events and discoveries.

Tree Secretly wished she could do just as her winged friends and fly about, soaring freely through the open skies. The ability to fly around and visit the many wondrous sites and of Eden was a fantasy; a dream that Tree knew would never come true. Some days she resented her station feeling very much confined to spend eternity plotted in one place. It felt strange, and rather unfair to Tree that she was made an inanimate object subject to watch as other creatures walked, ran and frolicked freely around her. The act of being a tree seemed cruel and unusual to her, and though Tree never dared to question or flaw the architect for her design, she still retained in her heart the dream of animation. Tree had long accepted the private dreams and fantasies that occupied space in her mind could only exist in her imagination. These intrusive thoughts and fantasies were often short lived, quickly thwarted away by the invisible hands of empathy. Tree reserved grace and compassion in her character accepting her invaluable position and role in maintaining the land and ecosystem. It was true that Tree held an indispensable and crucial role, serving as a vital instrument and resource. Tree was in a sense the foundational bridge that connected all creatures to life on earth. There was no other entity or creation that sacrificed more to the preservation and longevity of the royal garden than Tree. At the time there was no one kinder, and more generous than Tree. Her unselfish and giving nature revealing as to why all the creatures of the land revered her.

They birds flew down and perched themselves atop the sturdy canopy and limbs of Tree's and leafy branches. It wasn't long before one of the birds drew a gawking gasp; the second bird spotted the small creature and gave out a similar cry. "Um, excuse me Tree, "said Crane, nervous and freighted "did you know that there is a beastly creature on top of your head?" "Yes!" echoed Heron, "Goodness, my friend," Crane retorted, "I do not recall having ever seen such a creature..." "Yes, but I have," interrupted Heron "it's obvious this creature, is a... no wait, its an... um...," Heron paused briefly to examine the creature leering over the defenseless creature perplexed in confusion. "Ha!" mocked Crane, "you don't know what it is! You always say you know what something is when you don't know..." "but I do...," answered Heron, "It's obvious by looking at its large head, and ears, that the creature is some kind of, hairless monkey of some sort." Tree gave out a faint snicker and tried desperately to hold back the growing urge to laugh. Tree listened on in amusement as the two friends carried about their nonsensical bickering. "A hairless monkey???" Crane mocked laughably. "Why, yes!" answered Heron, "I am almost, positively certain that it is." "Except its tail is on the other side." Crane noted. The two birds gawked questionably over the strange creature's anatomy baffled and somewhat puzzled. Crane and Heron were proud creatures highly regarded by others for their vast wisdom and knowledge of the lands. The two were vastly familiar with the many species creatures residing in Eden. Their popularity went unmatched as the two birds collectively held acquaintances with nearly every creature living in Eden. However, the unknown creature placed before them seem to draw complexity and confusion over the pair.

Heron growing rather perplexed gave out a cry of frustration, "What sort of creature is this?" He questioned incessantly no longer able to bear the weight of his ignorance. "This creature does not make sense physiologically!" "Oh, stop it Heron," laughed Crane, "you'll startle the poor thing." Their eyes were glued with peaking interest over the small creature, "It's kind of cute if you ask me." Crane retorted playfully, with Heron responding disagreeably in disgust. Tree decided it best to assist her friends by providing them with the answers pertaining the strange and unfamiliar creature.

"I will explain it all soon," said Tree, "but first you must go throughout the kingdom and inform all our friends and family that they are being summoned this morning," Crane and Heron seemed somewhat confused by Tree's request, "Find every animal and creature," Tree continued "and tell them that we are having congregation here at noon and that God, demands every creature to be in attendance." The two birds glanced quickly at one another, and though they were filled with many questions, the sense of urgency in Tree's voice detoured them from imposing any further inquiries. The birds quickly flew away to do as Tree requested moving quickly to deliver the important message.

8

The Gathering

The sun engulfed and filled a quarter of the morning sky. The birds flew quickly through the land to deliver Tree's message. It wasn't long before the entire kingdom received the message. Some creatures arrived earlier than instructed with hopes of gaining a respectable vantage point. Some came excited, while others came tired, and grumpy, unaccustomed to being up so at such early hours. Creatures arrived from their homes, marching through the grassy terrain. The vast number of creatures in attendance resembled that of a disorganized parade.

Time was passing slowly, and the animals were becoming rather anxious. Tree, refused to speak or address the crowd until the sun had settled high into the sky, indicating that it was indeed noon. From high above Tree, watched as the creatures bunched together in clusters. The fashionable latecomers arrived squeezing through the crowd offering their petition and pardons before finding their proper seating. Heron, and Crane brought with them more winged birds and fair feathered friends. The birds soared through the sky and landed with a wild gust of wind over the crowd.

The sight was truly amazing with every animal in attendance except the water creatures but Tree, was confident the subject of the meeting would reach their ears. The bright sun shone over the faces of the massive crowd. Tree could see the sparkling gleam in their eyes twinkling like shards of crystals before the radiant sun. Tree panned

34

over the glittering faces for some time until eventually she was unable to differentiate individual creatures from the neighbor beside them.

Tree did not like speaking publicly and began to grow uncomfortable standing before the massive crowd. She began to question herself wondering whether she could overcome her fear and go through with it. Tree wished for more time, but knew it was too late as the moment had finally drawn near. Like a large sundial Tree's body cast a large shadowy indication that aligned perfectly in place with the sun. This in turn offered the impatient crowd an acute sense of time and understanding that noon was upon them.

The hot sun stood blazing its warm rays over the anxious crowd. It was safe to assume that all the creatures summoned, were present. Tree was surrounded and could hear the unsettling heckles from various directions. Tree found herself growing more nervous than before. "What is the meaning of this?" shouted an angry voice from within the crowd. A second voice cried out "Yea! What is going on? Where is God?" an uproar of grievances was beginning to stir within the crowd. There was an unspoken assumption gathered by the crowd possibly gathered and lost in communication and translation. The kingdom gathered with the expectation of being greeted by their king. The creatures were growing more impatient to the idea of his absence. "It's a trick!" shouted a voice in the crowd. Tree could see that she was beginning to lose control of the crowd and knew that she would need to act quickly if she wanted to settle the group.

Tree quickly shed her fears and took the center stage. She was ready to commence, "hello" Tree said softly, "as you know I am Tree," she paused, and peering into the crowd, she found the creatures inattentive and distracted. Mostly engrossed in their own chatter and affairs unaware that Tree had begun speaking. The few who held interest in her speech, struggled to hear her voice over the incessant chatter of their neighbors. Private conversations and frivolous dialogues, held by the crowd overpowered that of her own voice. The noise grew so loud that Tree could no longer hear her own thoughts amongst the loud chatter. Feeling flustered, and somewhat annoyed at the poor display before her, she fell silent.

Tree did not want to compete against the loud and out of control crowd. Staring silently over the crowd, she was able to spot the faces of various creatures waiting patiently, mindful and poised with loyalty and respect. Other faces flushed with annoyance irritated by the daunting heat. A strange feeling overcame Tree looking over the somewhat irritated crowd. The feeling produced a humbling smirk that began to form over her face. She relished for a moment at the thought that the entire garden was at present waiting to hear her speak. A strong sensation evoked suddenly within Tree, the combination of confidence and, determination that allowed her to dissolve her irrational fear of public speaking. Tree was no longer plagued with the urge to remain docile and silent.

"We are gathered here today!" yelled Tree, in a loud and powerful voice that could not be ignored. The blaring sound of her voice could not be ignored as the creatures quickly ended their private conversations turning their attention over to Tree. The tamed crowd behaved calmly with creatures in the crowd offering their silence and turning their focus over to the announcer. Tree continued with her speech, this time choosing to reduce the bass and manner she carried her voice. Tree would make the mistake of reverting back to the soft sound of her natural tone. This audible shift served to be problematic to the restless crowd who began to clutter and clammer with inaudible confusion. They were unable to clearly hear the details of Tree's announcement and began to regress returning once again to their previous state of senseless chattering.

The rear audience could scarcely make out or hear Tree's speech, while the elder more seasoned creatures struggled with their senses to make out her words. "What did she say?" Asked an old tortoise, to another, "I do not know!" answered the friend. Together the deaf stricken creatures harmonized their plea requesting that Tree to speak up, "Louder!" the crowd chanted together. Tree was revisited once again by the paralyzing emotions experienced just moments before. Her flaring spirit began to grow more intense in response to the increasing call to speak up. Tree understood that she could no longer speak softly but would have to project and amplify her voice to extend beyond her naturally timid persona, into that of a confident public figure and speaker.

This hoisting revelation helped to elevate Tree above the pinnacle of her fears. Tree still felt somewhat apprehensive and filled with anxiety around accepting her newly assigned position of power. The burden of stress that Tree carried on her shoulders began to deflate releasing her from her troubles and worries. There was a new sense of assurance that accompanied Tree's tone in addressing the crowd. Every word that escaped her diaphragm retained within it a haughty degree of dignity and arrogance. These qualities seem to resonate with the crowd serving as the foundational pillars of mutuality the essential cornerstones of dignity and respect.

9

The Prophecy

"A great conflict has arrived in our kingdom!" Tree sounded off, no longer questioning the intensity of her own voice. "His lordship has granted me permission to speak candidly regarding the chaos and corruption that is developing above in the heavens." The crowd simmered down to hear clearly the important news being brought to them by Tree. "God says the only thing that can save the heavens is his most recent creation, a creature he calls, Man!" The crowd appeared rather puzzled wearing blank looks of confusion faces looking up at Tree. The crowd struggled to comprehend the gravity, and severity of her message. The creatures shot glances back and forth at one another as if expecting to find resolve and resolution drawn on the faces of their fellow mates. The desperate search for reassurance concluded with the crowd reflecting similar looks of void and confusion. "The life and welfare of this of this new creature," Tree continued, "will depend on our cooperation and support. The burden and responsibility of rearing this new creature will fall on us all. It shall be the common duty of all those residing in garden to ensure the safety, and livelihood of this creature. This means that we must all work together to nurture, maintain, and rear this creature as though the creature were one's own creed or kin. It goes without objection that each of us must accept the proposed agreement and submit our consent to safeguarding the new infant creature."

Tree concluded her lengthy address to the crowd. "The message was direct, yet not too imposing," Tree thought to herself looking over at the audience that seemed somewhat numbed and stunned by the announcement. The bewildering silence of the deafened crowd was all but short lived as prevailing discord and chaos began to ensue. A wave of outcries poured openly from the contemptuous crowd who appeared rather flustered and un-flattered to receive the assignment of serving as God parents to the new creature.

A host of unsavory words, and comments were heard echoing deep within the bowels of the morbid crowd. It was safe to assume that many of the creatures were unhappy with the abrupt, and somewhat earth-shattering news. The crowd began to unravel quickly with many creatures shouting and behaving disorderly amongst their peers. Each creature felt eager to voice their displeasure, and discontent. Tree was growing uncertain whether to credit the creatures unsettling response as being a natural reaction to the shocking and somewhat intrusive news. Tree was empathetic to the creatures who were now filled with mixed emotions after being blindsided and stunned by shocking proposal. "It is our kings request," Tree stammered, "It is God who commands it not I." Tree pleaded desperately before the irritable crowd, but no one seem interested in hearing her appeal.

The creatures groaned, and roared, moaned and thumped trampling about wallowing in self-pity, and sorrow. Tree decided it best to allow the creatures a moment to process their feelings of frustration. The brief intermission would offer the tempered crowd an outlet and a much-needed opportunity to sooth their fiery tempers and lay down their emotional pitchforks. The creatures carried out their protest through public display behaving inconsiderably wild and untamed. It seemed as if every animal was somehow personally offended by the announcement and complained, voicing their contempt and outrage to their neighbors. However enraged or upset by the decree not a single creature dared to speak out directly in objection of the sacred request ordered by the king.

Their kings' indisputable commands were deemed difficult if not impossible for any group or individual to refuse. The hubris act of defying the king would constitute as a form of treason punishable by way of isolation and alienation, often time resulting in discharge from Eden. Tree could easily report any group that dared to refuse or any individual unwilling to participate and comply with the requested task. The already dense atmosphere appeared to grow more tense. The crowd seem to be displeased, and less delighted at the news of having been assigned such loathsome work. Sensing the hostile emotions of the crowd dwindling, Tree decided now was the best time to intervene and offer some refreshing words to sooth the parched and irritated crowd.

"It is I" shouted Tree, "your true and noble friend standing before you today, solemnly imploring your support, and assistance. I plea for your mercy and beg for your aide in completing such an undertaking and hefty task. I understand your grief, and I too share similar concerns, however it is a burden that we all must bear and share in together. I am unable to manage this great feat alone without your help. Just think of the great joy it will bring our king if we are able to succeed and fulfill this request." A few creatures smiled at the thought of pleasing their king, while others rolled their eyes and sucked their teeth's signifying their indifference and lack of interest in pleasing a remote and absent king.

The crowd began to chatter amongst themselves in low whispers. Tree was appalled by the creatures conduct and blatant display observing the lack of regard being shown by her fellow creatures. The crowd was growing restlessly impatient as some creatures began to prance about freely, roaming, and socializing with others. At first their low whispers, muffled and indistinguishable grew gradually turning into loud incoherent chatter. Some animals riled on franticly, grouped together in large clumps. The unanimous sentiment commonly shared at the time were feelings of concern and confusion being expressed amongst the crowd. The creatures all seemed to compete for the ears and attention of their neighbor beside them. The creatures turned to one another to unload their many disapprovals and personal grievances to the closest creature who would listen. The incessant noise of the crowd increasing steadily began to grow out of control once again. Tree was slowly losing her grip over her audience no longer able to tame or manage the disorderly mob. The creatures behaved as though Tree had somehow ended the service prematurely and vanished suddenly. Many of the creatures began to commune and congregate speaking freely amongst their friends and neighbors.

Just then a loud disagreement broke out within the crowd, that quickly escalated into heated argument. Two creatures with opposing views began to squabble openly before the large crowd and audience. The heated disagreement drew on, growing more intense and distasteful in their conduct and behavior. Their voices flared back and forth at one another, each yelling and shouting unkind words at the other. What should have been a private and personal disagreement had now spilled over infecting over the crowd contaminating groups of their and nearby surrounding creatures. Heavy growling and roaring outcries prepared the scene for a beastly rumble. The two creatures who seem to be equally matched in mass, and strength began tussling, and thrashing one other. They drew encouragement from the attention and excitement gathered by the crowd eagerly cheering them on rather than attempting deescalate the feud. The roaring crowd only helped to further fuel the fiery flames of the two fighters by offering words of encouragement to the rivals as they wrestled each other to the ground. The crowd cheered on with amusement finding great entertainment in viewing such gruesome exhibition. The utter display of disrespect was highly undignified and rather upsetting for Tree to watch or bare witness. It was apparent that the creatures were no longer concerned with the issue at hand, but were rather engulfed in satisfying their primal urge, and instinct to compete, argue and fight.

The rude behavior, and blatant display of disrespect brought a tense and somewhat anguishing feeling over Tree. She looked somberly down over at the crowd gathered before her with humiliation, and embarrassment. She listened sorrowfully as a tedious arguments began to flare and break out amongst different member of the crowd. Tree heard bickering amongst the primed and youthful creatures teasing one another over simple and trivial matters. "Zebra, you have yet to figure out, whether you are black, or white?" laughed lady Gazelle to her complicit friends Tortoise, and Hare as they all laughed together.

"Well, my mother tells me that I am white," answered Zebra, "and I believe her, then again, my father tells me that I am black, and I believe him as well." "You are so confused!" teased the menacing triad giggling and laughing at Zebra. It wouldn't be long before the small group of instigators were joined in by others in laughter.

The tension finally reached its toll becoming too much for Tree to sit idly. Tree was growing rather frustrated and contentious by what she was witnessing and began to draw a heavy gust of air into her lungs. Had anyone been paying the slightest attention to Tree they would have been able to foresee the inevitable outcome and somehow brace themselves for the loud deafening outcry that was getting ready to follow. "Enough!!!"

10

The Prophecy Cont.

"Enough! I said," Tree shouted repeatedly. The intensity of her demand startled the creatures, catching them all by surprise. The sheer power and intensity of her voice was heard throughout the garden. Her strained nerves quaked uncontrollably so intense that it startled many of the birds and caused them to fly away and flee in panic and distress. It was the tone in Tree's voice that echoed sending a shudder through the audience seizing their attention. The crowd froze instantly, not a single creature moved. They all stood stunned, and somewhat amazed by the loud thunderous noise that rung in their ears. Many of the creatures looked on puzzled and bewildered unable to believe that it was Tree who produced such a piercing outcry.

Tree was upset as her voice was no longer docile, or meek. It raged with power and surged with pride. The smaller creatures, alongside the elderly animals felt unsettled, unnerved by Tree's behavior. The older more mature creatures wished for nothing more than for this frightening meeting and ordeal to conclude so that they could return to their homes. The youthful adults being more skeptical, and opinionated than those of their elders were short tempered and were easily offended and outraged that Tree would speak to them in such a harsh tone and manner. The situation appeared to be grim for Tree, who was simply attempting to fulfill her master's wishes.

All the creatures of the Eden generally liked tree, and found her to be wholesome, and earnest. She was regarded for her qualities such as being kind, generous, and polite. She was utterly delightful and joy to keep company. But in the present moment Tree did seem to be her usual self and was behaving tempered and unsympathetically cruel. It appeared to the crowd as thought she had renounced her reputation of kindness, and generosity for a firmer and more serious persona.

Tree's new attitude and demeanor seem unbefitting of natural character, however being firm served an effective tool of intervention. The creatures were no longer bickering, or squabbling amongst themselves, and instead directed all their anger and frustration in her direction. Tree was unprepared for the flagrant backlash of verbal assaults received from the contemptuous crowd. They spun and hurled foul and unflattering insults aimed to belittle and tear down Tree's confidence severing her from her newly elevated sense of righteousness. Initially it appeared as though their trolling comments insults unfriendly words had no impact or effect over the grand matriarch, but over time their cruel words began to erode and chip away at her armor of confidence as she struggled to recover the fiery tone in her voice. It wouldn't be long before Tree, would find herself subdued by the overwhelming heckles being produced by the ill-mannered and out-of-control crowd.

It was the actions of her two close friends, and acquaintances Panther, and Tiger who had been nearby, and watching their friend, frantic, and failing miserably in her attempt to settle the anxious and rowdy crowd. The two friends sought to help Tree by intervening and offering their assistance with regaining control of the unruly crowd. "What is the matter dear old friend," Panther cried out while playfully prowling back and forth before agitated crowd. "Yes!" agreed Tiger, "you do not seem to be your usual joyful high-spirited self today. Tree is everything alright?"

Of all her creatures living in the garden, Tree was relieved to find that her closest feline friends had rallied to her rescue. Panther, and Tiger were respected figures well known and celebrated as two of the fastest and strongest creatures that lived in all of Eden. "Everything is fine," Tree attempted to reassure her friends, but unable to mask her frustration, "no, truthfully, I am a bit flustered today," Tree, answered honestly, "I only wish to complete the task commanded by our king, but this daunting request would be utterly impossible task to fulfill without the garden's assistance and support." "Is there anything we can do to help?" asked Panther, looking up at her companion and friend. "Yes" Tree replied, "would it be possible to settle the crowd so that I may complete my speech?" "No problem," answered Tiger, "we can manage that for you. Together Tiger, and Panther, growled and snarled, snatched and scratched, until the crowd finally settled down. The fiery crowd began to simmer down growing surprisingly obedient and respectfully attentive before presence of their honored speaker.

Tree thanked her two feline companions for their support and continued with her speech. She looked on, at the docile crowd, and waited as the last mouth was silenced by the shooing of their neighbor. Tree was content with the soothing silence that fell before her. She was assured, and convinced that her message would resonate, and be accepted and carried as the direct will and command of their king.

"As I was saying before," Tree began again "our all and mighty powerful king. God has created a new creature, one that he believes to be by far his greatest works. And upon witnessing the creation for myself, I somewhat agree that the creature is a rather unique and interesting creation." Growing interest, and excitement began to build from the crowd. "Our King says that he has created this new creature, in the image of himself, and in a way gifted onto us a part of himself it may seem." Tree was building on the momentum of the crowd. And it was working; the once enraged and combative audience were now fixated and filled with anticipation and good spirits after receiving Tree's report.

The garden seemed to wail with joy as many more animals joined in the excitement, The birds chirped, and shrieked loudly, while the bears and wolves and other creatures sounded their approval with howls and growls to demonstrate their enthusiasm. As it stood the new creature was now being welcomed into the garden with ushering acceptance. It was only after the noises had settled down, did different voices began to pick up. One senior patron standing near the forefront called out cheerfully, "Man! God has given unto us, Man!" Another creature joined in, "Yes, a creature of his likeness, in what way?" A third voice spoke out, "Show us Man!" The request was infectious with other creatures quickly joining in. Another creature from the crowd yelled out, "What does Man look like? Is the creature here?" Requests to meet man, rang out from all ends of the crowd, "Show us, man!" The creatures quickly adopted the new mantra and chimed together in perfect harmony their growing interest in meeting the newly renowned creature.

The loud and obsessive requests to meet the new creature was heard throughout the flourishing garden. The noise produced by the overly enthusiastic crowd was deafening and began to make Tree feel uncomfortable and uneasy once again. Tree began to feel herself losing momentum and control over the impatient crowd, however this time she was determined to retain the crowd, refusing to relinquish her attentive hold over the massive audience. Tree began to exhale slowly exhausting a heap of air from her lungs only to draw back into her body in heaping gust of air. The alarming gesture caused distress amongst the audience with many responding instinctively to cover or plug their ears. The crowd was prepared to embrace another piercing outcry from their impatient host. Luckily it was Panther, and Tiger who gave out a loud growl that served as the necessary prompt and cue for the crowd to settle down. The creatures were immediately silenced just in time for Tree shift the intensity of her outcry into a gusty sigh of exhaustion. The breath of fresh air was felt over the crowd like a draft being carried by the gusty wind. A tepid sense of reassurance fell over the audience with many in the crowd feeling relieved that Tree did not scream or shout at them.

Tree continued her speech reassuring her listeners. "All will be revealed, if I am permitted to conclude my announcement without facing a barrage of senseless interruptions." The bold statement appeared to draw the respect and admiration of some crowd members who reacted enthusiastically with cheering applauds. It seemed somehow Tree was being celebrated for her candid straightforwardness. The crowd rejoiced with excitement after learning of the upcoming conclusion and end to Tree's lengthy speech. They quickly stabilized themselves without requiring any cue's or prompting from Panther or Tiger. They returned their attention back over to Tree to conclude and finisher her announcement. Tree retained her dignified poise and civil tone.

"My friends and fellow neighbors I will soon reveal onto you the creature man. But first I feel that I must first disclose my obligation to this creature in accordance with the royal doctrines of the land. Hence, I will provide a summary that will provide context and answer questions surrounding the conditioning of the new creature. And though my analysis maybe somewhat informal and presumptuous our mighty lord has deemed it necessary that I provide a grand and celebratory indoctrination of the new breed." Tree looked around at all the gleaming faces staring anxiously up at her. She was overcome with a sense of notoriety looking down at the attentive faces staring up at her. "My dear friends, this new creature is coveted!" Tree announced firmly. A loud gasp drew from the mouths of the crowd. "God, our lordship and master has chosen to embed within the soul and spirit of this new creature a substantially large portion of his own power and will into this new creation and being called, Man. God has forged man to help assist in fulfilling the king's prophecy."

Whispers began to stir, within the crowd, as the animals shot confused glances back and forth at another "pro-phi-cy?" repeated the creatures growing worried by the unfamiliar word and began chattering amongst themselves. It was only Antelope, who was bold enough to inquire upon the word, and dared to interrupt Tree. In a meek and tiny voice, the inquisitive creature spoke as if embarrassed to speak out and voice his inquiry publicly. Antelope faced his fears before the crowd at the risk of being labeled dunce and asked, "Tree, what is a prophecy?" A fleeting sense of anger and frustration over came Tree who feeling somewhat flustered by the audacity of Antelopes intrusive inquiry.

It was believed to be true that younger generation of creatures that lived in Eden were not well-versed in the word and language of God despite being their king and creator. They struggled to recall the very image of God, with very few who could offer testimonial accounts and interaction of meeting their king. As a result of his extended absences and sabbatical God was now being regarded by youthful generation as folklore told to them during their infantile stage. The younger generation accepted the notion of God as deriving from stories shared and passed down to them as traditional stories shared by their elders.

Tree nearly overlooked Antelope intrusive question, but stop short, and decided it best to answer the poor creature's inquiry. Tree couldn't explain it, but suddenly, she felt a sense of urgency, and obligation to educate the youth, and teach them their forgotten history as well help unify their bond with their mighty creator. Aside from the youth, Tree looked over at the many confused faces in the crowd and was overcome with the nagging suspicion that Antelope was not the only creature possibly struggling to decipher the unfamiliar term prophecy and exactly what that word entailed.

"A prophecy," began Tree, "is a binding promise that one must keep in respects to the linear direction of their fate. It is the preordained assignment and direction of one's life, and destiny. It is one's calling, or better yet one's own awakening and actualization. It is an honorable and purposeful role and position designed by his all mighty. It is ultimately a garnered path that must be assumed and followed within in one's lifetime. With it being equally important to understand that not all prophecies are contractual, or indispensable. Some prophecies can become fallible and go undiscovered if not supported by the discretionary hands of chance and luck."

The creatures drew out heavy breaths of sighs expressing a state of relief after being presented with the clarity and understanding surrounding the unfamiliar and strange term. The creatures became ecstatic once again as cheers filled the air indicating they were happy in not satisfied by Tree' response. The discovery that no creature's life or home was at risk or jeopardy was quickly received with rejoicing celebration from the crowd. The present situation appeared to the crowd as an ominous event; a day of celebration and good fortune, especially when considering the latter of worsening possibilities and outcomes. The creatures riled up once again with excitement this time crying out, and pleading for Tree to continue, "tell us more" they chanted out, harmonizing in their request. Tree could easily observe by the crowd's growing embrace and response deducing that they were once again receptive to welcoming the new man creature into Eden. Tree rejoiced at the thought of their conviction and prepared to conclude her assignment. The introduction and summary of man was nearly halfway complete.

Tree looked over the crowd waiting patiently in revering silence for her to continue and hopefully complete the prolonged speech. She was filled with an overwhelming sense of joy and admiration standing before the large crowd. Quickly stealing a moment for herself Tree imagined herself as a queen standing before an audience of her loyal and faithful subjects. Her heart swelled with immeasurable pride, imagining herself not as the host but the central figure of this event. Tree was pretending as though that the large reception was being held in her honor with everyone gathered to celebrate her work and crowing achievements. The idea and notion that she could evoke joy and arouse admiration from her peers served as a triumphant win and cause for celebration.

"When the time is right, the creature shall grow and become our powerful ruler. The creature will guide, and lead us, in transforming

Eden into a vast and boundless utopia. Imagine a world, without the need of borders or grand walls, and endless green pasture as far as the eyes can see, or legs can travel." The audience stood mesmerized and amazed submerged and lost at the mercy of their own imaginations. The crowd were snagged, lassoed in by Tree's majestic gift and use of language. "This new creature will live and grow with us, and in return we will nurture and protect it. And if executed correctly, I believe that man will grow to regard us dearly and retain within him the equitable devotion to nurture and protect us." Smiles, and cheers, filled the faces of the audience members. Tree tried desperately to remain focused, but often found herself distracted by the loud reception of applauding and rallying cheers. "Thank you," Tree repeated to the crowd joyfully, and had she been granted the ability of animation, or flexibility Tree would have surely bowed, and curtsied before her adoring public.

Tree, continued with her speech with newly developed sense of confidence, and dignity. "Fellow, friends, I will not stand before you today, and act as though I know the full telling of this new creature's life, however there will come a day when man will be summoned to fulfill its destiny. At present I understand that man is destined to reign over heaven and earth at the side of our master and lord, God." Cheers rang out from the crowd at the very mention of their king's name. "This new creature," Tree continued, "will be destined for either monumental greatness, or serve as an instrument of misfortune and peril." The crowd was a bit shaken, and taken back, "I have said all this only to conclude with this warning," Tree added quickly, "Man has been gifted, or rather somewhat cursed with the element of free will. The audience grew more intrigued, and curious about the new creature. "Man's imagination will exceed beyond the depths of the ocean floor, and with similar effort it will scale unprecedented heights with unforeseen potential elevating him into peaks of the heights." Tree commended her-self on her fanciful use of wordplay, not before looking down at her audience who no longer appeared amused or in good spirits.

Tree's complex description of man began to stir within the crowd mixed sentiments surrounding the legitimate anointing of such an immaculate being. The creatures appeared less enthusiastic and more concerned by the boundless prospect of man's potential capabilities. The growing tension and divide being mostly baseless having been derived and concocted from the infancy of their own imaginations. The creatures reserved feelings of nervousness about their eventual ruler who they took to be in his description a wild, tentacled monstrous creature that drank from ocean beds and scoured mountain tops. The crowd had never met or been introduced to such an abominable creature. The creatures in Eden had never once heard of such phrases and words such as "curiosity", and "imagination". These foreign concepts appeared to them as being arbitrary, and senseless. The imposition of such radicle ideas evoked resistance and hesitation within the minds and hearts of many audience members.

The residents of Eden at the time had no use for what they called fantasy ideology and propaganda. They had long since accepted the circumstances of their lives and very existence as impermeable and unchangeable. The tenants of Eden lived relatively simple lives and were simplistically content with the current standards and present status quo of the garden. Not a single creature had ever desired or thought to consider the idea of change or being anything other than their design. The very concept was unfathomable, with many believing the act to be utterly impossible beyond their will. The creatures removed themselves from the supernatural reigns of existentialism, abandoning ideas of creativity and leaving the work of imagining solely up to God. They took solace in accepting their king to be a just, and fair master who serves in the interest and benefits of his subjects. The creatures of Eden believed unquestionably in the benevolence of their omnipotent creator. In their eyes God was observed as kind and virtuous in accordance with the principle's righteousness.

There was a shared belief that God only permitted the necessary and good of things to cultivate and grow in Eden, while withholding and removing whatever he deems as inappropriate and unnecessary. As far as the inhabitants of the Eden were concerned, they were happy with the present order and state of the world. The creatures never thought or troubled themselves with curiosity or considered the idea of a new world outside their current reality. The creatures at the time who were all animals lacked the natural curiosity and inclinations that was inherited by man. However, in their defense at the time the creatures had very little desire or need know the what's, why's and how's of the world extending beyond the boundaries of their home. In their limited scope and view they believed nowhere else existed and that nothing could exist outside of Eden.

Tree, paused briefly to allow the crowd a moment to settle down and regain their composure. She paced herself patiently while gauging the sounds of mummers and whispering developing among the crowd. Tree that was losing her hold and grip over the crowd, she realized that it was imperative that she regain control of her audience. Her lengthy roots extending deep beneath the ground could sense through vibrations growing anxiety and nervousness of the collective crowd. Tree's speech unintentionally provoked fear and concern from the audience. The chattering noise slowly softened eventually falling into deafening silence. At present there was no other voice more significant or consequential than that of the current speaker. Tree demonstrated patience and understanding surrounding the buildup of tension and uneasiness displayed by the alarmed and fearful crowd. They appeared somewhat mournful and perplexed rather eager if not anxious for Tree to carry on with the conclusion of her speech. Her every word hung like sweet supple nectar before a depraved and famished crowd.

11

The Unveiling

"We can never begin to imagine the hidden powers that lay dormant within the frame and body of the new creature called man." Tree cautioned. "Man is unlike any other creature before us today for within this creature presides the very will, and essence of God. The creature harnesses the ability to create, destroy, and rebuild as it sees fit. Man will one day bridge the world between heaven and earth giving new breadth and meaning to life and the notion of existence." The audience listened with bewildered astonishment and could not believe that such a creature that could exist possessing such power and potential for elevated greatness. A flood of mixed emotions soon engulfed the crowd as they listened on. It was easy to see that some of the creatures were uncomfortable with the idea of any creature-harnessing similarly godlike potential and power. The creatures wore looks of mystified skepticism, shooting glances back and forth at one another as if in search of a brave soul or martyr willing to stand up and speak out voicing their discontent on the matter.

The audience appeared to be troubled and conflicted once again by Tree's report. They wore dreary looks of concern and disapproval over their despairing and concerned faces. The creatures no longer felt warm, and welcoming to the prophecy, and were already beginning to put into question the dramatic exaggeration of man's power. The crowd struggled with managing their intrusive thoughts and growing sense of inferiority. The creatures feared the idea and implication that a divine creature possessing the might and will of God, could ultimately alter the very fabric and dynamic of their culture and society.

Tree was conscious of the crowd's apprehension and growing concerns. The vibration of their fears and worries still trembling beneath the ground. Fear and trepidation were not the emotions that Tree was attempting to promote. She had no intention of steering her audience away from the path of acceptance into the path and direction of ambivalence and skepticism. The trembling ground beneath their feet shook nervously demonstrating their growing anxieties. "Be still my friends," Tree spoke reassuringly, "be tardy to entertain your worries and concerns. In these uncertain times it is imperative that we remain firm and strong in our values, and not give into the wallowing temptation of indignity and inadequacy." The vote of assurance brought with it sense of great relief over the audience causing many to confidently reclaim their value and self-confidence "This new creature is a blessing from God," Tree reminded them, "given onto us for having served our lord and master so honorably. God, has given man to us as a reward, like a shepherd amongst his faithful flock, one day man will watch over and care for, us."

Tree was determined to curate the best possible scenario by being hopeful in her outlook regarding the outcome and future of the Eden. The crowd now behaving attentively poised and composed were happily receptive to accepting Tree's positive and optimistic point of view. Her ideas seem to cast a blanket of reassurance over the crowd derailing them from their narrow minded and skeptical train of thought. Despite her present advocation Tree inwardly sided with the views and concerns expressed by her fellow friends and natives. She like many reserved private concerns regarding the potential fate and outcome of Eden as a result God's decision. Tree retained her private opinion over the unprecedented decision to appoint a creature especially that of a mortal into the highly ranked position of celestial ruler.

She had many questions and inquiries to pose but thought it best to proceed with the conclusion of the telling tale and prophecy of man.

"This new creature is gifted with an unbelievable mind, which will one day send him to the depths of the world in search of all its wonders. Man will travel far beyond the clouds and soar further than the world itself. The creatures seem to marvel in amazement, never giving much thought to such perilous wonders being described. "One day man will emerge," Tree added, "and conquer the moon, and eventually the stars, then on to whatever object that sunlight refracts and touches. Trust and believe my friends that man is well equipped and endowed, capable of achieving endless wonders and possibilities."

The crowd was stunned speechless, no one had ever dreamt of conquering the stars, or traveling the ends of the world. Interest and support for the creature was slowly being restored in the minds, and hearts of the animal kingdom. "This new creature" said Tree, hoping to conclude her speech, "will come to rule over the lands, and then the heavens. Let us all pray that man will be able to bring heaven down to Eden." The prophecy was finally complete, Tree, expected a reception of cheers from her endearing crowd, but instead found them irritated and unamused.

The audience looked on at Tree presumably overwhelmed by the prolonged meeting. Tree was empathetically compassionate that she had fast fed the crowd a mass amount of information but had not provided them the ample time necessary to fully digest and process the bits and pieces of her prophetic message. It became suddenly apparent by the alarming looks on all the creatures faces that Tree's speech had deeply impacted them. A mutual feeling of despair began to weigh over the crowd that seem to anchor their thoughts. They began once again to shift and dart their eyes back, and forth across an ocean of glooming faces. The distraught crowd overcome with numbing uncertainty how they should react to Tree's message. They turned their attention and faces in search of validation from their neighboring family and friends. Those that sought out familial and friendly faces were saddened to discover the faces reflecting similar looks of concern, and worry. The crowd growing noticeably withdrawn appeared internally conflicted by their sudden enrollment of their support. The loaded demand arrived as a humble request enveloped and addressed to a crowd who could neither refuse nor decline her request.

An unsavory odor suddenly filled the air, the foul and unpleasant stench demonstrated the collective discontent of the frightened and fearful onlookers. A crescendo of low whispers rushed over the crowd like gentle waves. The creatures muttered amongst themselves in screeches, and gawks, groans, growls, and moans, expressing their disapproval and uncertainty. Gorilla was the only creature that dared to speak out from amongst the crowd. "Never!!!" Gorilla cried out. His prideful refusal demonstrated his arrogance followed by an exuberant display of defiance by savagely beating against his chest. "Not me!" "Not I!" "Not ever!" It was easy to foresee the affect and influence that Gorillas rude rebellious and childlike temperament would have over the impressionable crowd. Instantly all the monkey's, orangutans, and primates riled together in joyful celebration. They mimicked noisily, Gorilla's words, shouting and wailing the phrase "Never, not I!" repeatedly. The gophers, ferrets and other ground critters expressed their disapprovals with sharp squeaks, and chirps, but found their wails, muffled by the loud voices, of the larger animals. The long-legged creatures turned away their snouts and stomped their hoofs and stampeded about signifying their disapproval. It was unanimously understood that the creatures disliked the telling prophecy of man. The creatures seem to recant their initial approval and acceptance of the new creature.

The creatures appeared displeased and unhappy to learn of man's role and assigned rank at the pinnacle. They now grasped with full comprehension the monumental change that was preparing to take place. The new creature would signify a new era, a shift in the hierarchy of the animal kingdom. The tension in the air was thick, and building with intensity, and frustration. All the creatures except

Tree, wore a look of anguish and disappointment. Tree seemed down-trodden with despair, and hopelessness. She had done as God, asked of her, and was unsure as to how she should proceed forth. The creatures no longer searched for reassurance amongst the crowed faces of their family and friends. The disappointed crowd misdirecting their frustration and began to behave more impolite and discourteous hurling insults and unkind words in her direction. The large crowd resembled that of an unorganized mob gathered in non-peaceful protest. They yelled and shouted out together, many issuing similar grievances and complaints demanding answers. The animals reacted immaturely and behaved poorly, they cursed and blamed the messenger for delivering such dreary and unfortunate news.

Tree was empathetic to the onslaught of their mistreatment; she regarded the crowd's behavior as nothing more than a natural re-action and response after being summoned to accept such an unex-pected burdensome request. Tree refrained from engaging directly with the upset and contentious crowd. Designed with the heightened ability to navigate emotional intelligence Tree was able to overcome the desire and impulse to challenge and defend her honor and repu-tation from the onslaught of scrupulous insults. Tree was unfazed by the matter and retaliated strategically by simply offering the irritated creatures a gentle reminder, "be mindful," she suggested in a calm as-suring voice, "that our lordship and king is omnipotent, and that he hears and sees all that we do." The creatures were instantly gripped with fear and flushed with embarrassment reflecting over their con-duct and behavior. They ceased their senseless chattering and settled down quietly waiting for Tree to offer consultation and guidance on the matter. The creatures somehow hoped that Tree could somehow produce a remedy to resolve this ordeal. "A kind and gracious host," Tree started "cannot bear to keep the company of an impolite and rude guest." looking over the many faces in the crowd, "I suggest in good faith my dear friends, that we watch our tongues, and pay our respects, unless we cherish not the weight of our dues."

"Tell us then Tree, what should we do?" Alligator asked. "What can we do?" Bear responded voicing their defeat. "I was not speaking to you" fired Alligator rather short tempered. Bear drew offense and was quickly irritated by Alligator's response. "Well, I'm telling you" Bear pushed back. Tree could already foresee the disagreement escalating especially with other creatures gathered around amplifying the growing conflict and feud between Alligator, and Bear. The entire incident seemed reminiscent to that of the previous ordeal that occurred just moments prior.

"Stop!!!" yelled Tree, "What are you doing?" she demanded to know, "Look at yourselves behaving wild and uncivil. We have lived peacefully together in this gardened paradise for centuries, we have come to call Eden our home, and today Eden welcomes a new creature into our home." Tree cleared her throat before proceeding further. "I before any other should fear this new creature most, for it is with me that this creature's life has been entrusted. It appears the creature and I are now connected one. The creature will live and be sustained through me and remain in my custodial care. I of course will assume primary responsibility and guardianship of man until the day God decides to return for his creation." Tree looked around at all the sunken faces looking up at her with sympathetic expressions of deep remorse and compassion for accepting such a strenuous and perilous assignment. "So, there you have it my friends, the ironic circumstances of my design and fate. I am expected to nurse, and care for, a creature that is most favored by his lordship. It is a most glorious honor and privilege to have bestowed by our lordship. It is a title and privilege for any creature to accept and happily fulfill."

Several annoyed creatures looked away and rolled their eyes in reaction to Tree's bold brazen remark. "I have come to accept this assignment as being either a test to my faith, or a punishment for some previous wrongdoing or offense. Either way my commitment in doing so will secure God's mercy and grace." Tree drew an awkward silence that seem to dimmish and quiet the crowd of onlookers who by this point were uncertain exactly how they should respond. A consensus of sympathy and relief fell over garden with all the animals expressing great relief after learning the details of Trees obligation and commitment to man.

The tepid feelings of hostility, and aggression reserved by the audience transformed instantly into feelings of remorse. A sense of relief fell over the crowd after learning of their supportive roles with Tree assuming the primary role of caretaker of man and carrying the bulk of responsibility and debt. It became apparent to the crowd that their petty conflicts and differences seemed trivial in comparison to the burdening load and responsibility being entrusted to Tree. The crowd appeared to sympathize with Tree looking on at her with pity and remorse for being thrust into such a compromising position. Several creatures gave thought and consideration to the plausible idea that Tree was somehow being punished and if so, on what account? What heinous crime had she committed deserving of such cruel and unusual punishment?

The long and uncomfortable silence in the air was disturbed by Beaver, who shouted from within the heart of the crowd, "Tree... how does this new creature look... does it have a long tail? You know what they say... the longer the tail the shorter the brain." Beaver joked openly.

Most of the animals' burst out into laughter, all except for the felines, who were instantly offended. Suddenly, Panther gave out a terrifying loud growl that quickly hushed and silenced the wild crowd. Tree called out to Giraffe requesting her assistance with retrieving the creature.

Giraffe walked down the aisle as instructed, she strutted her long legs moving delicately and gracefully through the crowded path. The extension of her long neck gave Giraffe an advantageous view of the world that many creatures openly envied and admired. Giraffe approached Tree and waited patiently for further instructions.

"Giraffe my friend, could you assist by bringing the creature down so that we may all become acquainted with our prince. "The creature is resting comfortably atop the base of my bulky crown. Please help bring the man creature down." Giraffe was happy to fulfill Tree's request and used her long neck to reach high up into Tree's lofty branches. Giraffe maneuvered her head back and forth in effort to safely secure creature. She struggled at first but recovered quickly, tucking her horns beneath the creature frame and delicately brought the creature down from its cozy bed of soft cotton leaves.

The audience filled with deafening silence, as they gazed on with great shock, and astonishment at the initial discovery and unveiling of man. The creatures tussled, pushing and shoving one another eager to catch a glimpse of the new creature. It was apparent that the unveiling of man was becoming a popular attraction. The audience became irritably entranced and fixated over the new creature. Many of the creatures began to crowd around and surround the creature. The pushed and shoved one another in search of an opening or space that would allow for a better view or closer look at the small creature. In this surprising moment the crowd's attention belonged to the strange and foreign creature placed before them. They studied the creature for some time examining the being with probing looks and unwavering speculations. The creatures appeared uncertain and unable to determine exactly what to make of the strange and usual creature called man. The creatures appeared mesmerized unable to draw their attention from the new creature. A unanimous sentiment of confusion was shared amongst the crowd puzzled in understanding how a frail and fragile creature could be assigned the noble destiny of becoming conquer of the world. It was challenging for the animals to view the small infant sized creature being superior. The creature possessed no distinctive traits or qualities which could measure up with the images drawn in their crowd's imagination. There was a sense of calm and relief after the reveal of man. The crowd blushed with embarrassment at the terrifying images they painted and drew up of man in their minds. Man was finally reveled to the crowd as the rightful heir to the heavenly kingdom. It was Tree, voice that broke the silent awkwardness of the trance like state of the crowd. Tree shouted out to her constituents in a loud and clear voice, "Lo, and behold! Man! Our master and new prince!"

The garden grew eerily silent; only the wind could be heard blowing about, skidding across the wavy grass. The wind blew with urgency, gusting quickly through the crowd, swaying past each animal swiftly as though eager to meet the new creature. The maneuvering wind unable to steady its gate lost balance and crashed directly into Tree. The collision sent an explosion of colorful leaves flying high into the air like fireworks. Leafy petal flew about cutting through the air like propellers before drifting slowly back down onto the ground. Tree found herself entangled by clumsy arms of the fumbling wind struggling desperately to free herself. The magical scene appeared intentionally orchestrated offering a celebratory unveiling and introduction of the new creature. The wonderful display was truly a spectacular production whether intentional accidental the entire scene was well-orchestrated and successful in climactically welcoming man into Eden. The crowd watched on with amusement as colorful leaves rain over them. Leaves flew about through the air, before spiraling slowly down to the ground. The unrehearsed shower was truly an amazing spectacle, and experience. Tree would not have been able to coordinate a better introduction or orchestrate a more fantastic reveal more spectacular than today's event.

A few remaining leaves drifted down over the new infant creature. The animals were captivated and brought to awe after hearing the strange sounds of shrieks and cooing being produced by the small creature. The tiny creature was undeniably adorable with its plump body and numerous folds adorable. The infant wore the cutest rearend on its backside, and possessed a natural charm that could disarm the most hostile of agitators. The sweet aroma of innocence filled the air whenever the creature, cooed or chuckled. The child easily captured the heart of any creature that happen to lay their sights beyond a glimpse. The creature's loud shrieks and piercing outcries were overlooked by its disarming smile which the creature happily plastered across its face. Very soon all the creatures found themselves under the creature's spell and enchantment. Mans fragile frame and utter display of helplessness enhanced the creature's attraction and appeal. The reception was successful in resolving Tree's concerns as to whether the creatures of the kingdom would offer their support and assistance with rearing the new creature. The gnawing concern of whether the garden would offer assistance and support was no longer a matter of uncertainty. All of Eden had instantly fallen in love with the new man creature, and took turns holding, and embracing the new creature. They displayed affection and tenderness toward the creature, sharing kind words and compliments filling the infant creature's ears with affirmations.

The creatures in the kingdom celebrated man by parading the small creature throughout the Kingdom for rest of the day. It wasn't until sunset that the parade ended, and the child was returned safely back home to Tree. And so, Tree thanked the wild creatures for welcoming the young prince into their kingdom. And just as Tree, was preparing to bid them all goodnight and farewell one of lady Duck's, youngest ducklings, stepped forth, and asked a question, concerning the new prince, "what is man's, name?", asked the young foul"

Tree paused at the question admitting to herself that she had not given much thought to the naming of the creature, for she had become content with calling the new creature man as his title. But at this moment Tree agreed that a worldly name would be beneficial and most useful in distinguishing the new unique creature. "But what name would suite a soon to be king" Tree thought, somewhat puzzled, "what name does one pose befitting the savior of the heavens, and earth. A being destined to bring an end to the flood of tyranny and evil like a dam..." "That's it!" thought Tree, "A dam, no Adam will be the creature's name from now on." Tree announced suddenly. "A'ddam." "Aa'dam, A,ddam? Adam!" mocked the young duck-lings, "well that's a silly name." laughed one the younger ducklings before quickly scurrying off just in time to evade their mother's rep-rimand. "Pardon my hatchlings Tree," apologized lady Duck, "Adam is a truly a beautiful name, very much appropriate and befitting for a prince and soon to be king." Lady Duck wished Tree, and the new prince now named Adam, a goodnight, before quickly hurrying to catch up with her young, Tree bid lady Duck, and everyone a Good-night, and a safe journey home.

That night the entire Eden slept peacefully with each creature se-cured in their home and dwelling. The cool nights air served like a thick blanket layered over the land helping the creature to fall asleep guiding their dreams into a world of bliss and endless possibilities. Eden was particularly quiet on this solemn night, with many of its creature and inhabitants already asleep. They dreamt of the many ways that they would serve the new prince and ultimately win favor and good fortune from the soon to be king. The creatures held firm to the hope that one day man would remember their effort and sup-port and in return demonstrate favor and generosity over the inhab-itants of the garden. These thoughts and more cradled their minds, rocking back and forth hypnotically like a pendulum. The symbolic instrument help to induce a prolonged and blissful state of rest and sleep over the garden.

12

The Becoming

Adam as the creature grew up to be called, was interestingly one of the most popular creatures in the kingdom. It was Adam's audacious exuberance that drew the interest and fascination of the other creatures. No animal had ever seen or met a creature quite as remarkable as the man creature. In his earliest years Adam would be described as a fearlessly bold creature often performing remarkable acts, and feats that no other creature dared to attempt. During the daytime Adam would be involved in childish play alongside the younger creatures of the garden.

As time went on Adam continued to develop and grow his name and eccentric personality was proceeded only by his reputation of bravery and boldness. They regarded Adam as the audacious one who raced alongside the wild mustangs to test his endurance and speed. Adam demonstrated his strength and might in competitions by challenging and wrestling apes and gorillas for sport. Adam was well versed in the practice of aquatics and often swam the rapid waters, side-by-side the sailfishes, and different sea urchins. Adam's tenaciousness outlook was the source of his pride and strength. No creature before man had ever dared or considered the idea of saddling backs of their fellow neighbors like the pesky tick and fly insects. The very notion seemed preposterous and deplorable, yet Adam was seen on many occasions straddling the backs and shoulders of the fiercest, and largest animals in the kingdom. As Adam's popularity and following increased so did his influence and notoriety grow in the garden. Adam was proclaimed for his reverence and highly esteemed for his politeness and humility seeming noticeably unfazed by his appointed royal status and title as prince. Adam's kind and gentle nature did not go unnoticed by those who encountered and interacted with him.

Wherever Adam ventured his name and reputation preceded him. He was met at various times of the day by different locals who would stop and go out of their way to greet him. "Why hello, Adam." "Hello," he would repeat back, often unsure as to the exact name of his greeter. Many times, the greetings came from familiar faces, while at other times he was met by unfamiliar faces of creatures who he had never seen or held acquaintances. The first time it happened, Adam brought the experience to Tree's attention. Adam explained how he had received numerous greetings, and compliments. "It seems that the entire garden knows who I am," Adam voiced his observation, "why is that so?" he asked innocently. Tree assured Adam, that the creatures in kingdom, meant him well, and were all in fact close acquaintances of his father. Adam was pacified, by Trees explanation, and afterwards was no longer bothered by the random number of new faces that greeted him daily. He now willingly accepted the creatures imagining them all to be familiar friends and associates of his father.

For a long time, everything in the kingdom was well, and Adam was content living amongst the creatures in Eden. The thought of being the son of a noble icon served and sustained Adam during his younger years, but as he grew older so would his yearning desire to meet his father. Adam dreamt of the day when he would be reunited with his father struggling internally with not being able to recall the face and image of his father and creator. Despite enduring the extended absence of his father Adam grew up to be reasonably well mannered and polite managing to maintain his credibility, and reputation intact for most of his young adult life. However, as Adam began to transition approaching the prepubescent stages of adulthood. He chartered the unfamiliar phase of adolescent with little guidance or mentorship. This caused Adam to experience a change in his mood and overall attitude. He drew skepticism and adopted a diminishing outlook and perspective on his legacy and often questioned the legitimacy of his foretold prophecy. It was apparent that Adam was distraught attempting to navigate the treacherous terrain of adolescence alone and began to give up on the thought and likelihood that his father and creator would ever return for him.

The childish exuberance which at one time or another help to fill Adam's spirt began to slowly wither and decay over time. The vacant void allowed for growth and maturity to form in its place. Adam was no longer a frolicking boy engaged in playful sport and childish games. He was no longer enthralled by reckless competitions or enticed by needless antics. Adam was different now, growing bolder it seemed in his range as his everyday strolls through the garden became more adventurous and filled with delightful new discoveries. Adam enjoyed the unrestricted access and freedom of walking through the garden and often ventured far and deep into the jungle. His natural curiosity encompassed his direction and steered his steps. Adam would be seen walking around the various areas of the garden. It was during these silent and lengthy walks that he gathered new ideas and reflected privately in deep thought.

One day a sudden revelation dawned over Adam as he was hiking through the forest. He often came across and encountered young animals in the company of their fathers. Some fathers played with their young, while others held their kin near and close to their bodies. Adam had often noticed these acts daily, but this moment watching the affectionate and warm display he became gripped with sadness. Taunted by these melancholy emotions Adam attempted to flee however useless was his attempt to escape. It appeared everywhere he ventured, he was met by dyads and triads of families displaying affection towards their young.

"Why am I not privileged..." thought Adam "where is my father, and why does he not hold me as tenderly as father Bear, holds his dear cubs. Why does my creator shun and neglect me so, by not keeping close watch over like the rumbling rams watch over their tender lambs."

Gazing over at his surroundings Adam began to pay close attention to the cluster of creatures as they gathered each night in groups of two or three's resembling that of a nuclear family. Adam confirmed this idea after observing the patterns and routine behavior of the animals. He observed the creatures and studied their habits with special interest and careful consideration to how they attended to the needs of their young. The longing revelation of belonging seem to stir and awaken dormant emotions and feelings of sorrow and loneliness in Adam's mind and heart. Adam grew up believing that all the creatures that inhabited the garden lived autonomously independent. Strangely he imagined that all the animals in Eden resided in their own separate space and dwelling. Adam never considered that beneath the surface of scattered herds their existed multiple groups of interdependent families. Adam stood frozen staring off into the furthest corners of his mind in deep contemplation of his circumstances. It never occurred to Adam that creators could covet their creations so tenderly. An instant numbing pain began to ache throughout Adam's body. The affectionate display triggered a sense of anguish and sadness within Adam that he was unable to comprehend, nor could he understand the rapturing emotions that grieved him. The intense feeling of despair became difficult to manage. Adam could only stare down at his feet no longer able to bare the weight of watching animals and other forest creatures tending to their young.

Adam was experiencing the sensation described as jealousy and envy for the very first time. He would not stir or budge for some time, plagued by a personal struggle of dueling thoughts and waring emotions. The victor of the internal conflict was made evident by the look defeat and sadness drawn on his face. The cups of his eyes began to swell and slowly fill with tears until finally it reached its tipping point and began to spill down his face. The first few drops help to wake Adam from his trance state. He reacted quickly in effort to stop the flood of tears by covering and masking his face. But it was too late, Adam could not hold back the flood of tears soaking through his palms running down his arm. Not knowing what else to do, Adam set off running fleeing as quickly as he possibly could to avoid being seen or probed with questions from onlookers. Adam ran deep into the woods in search of a quiet secluded area of the forest. He sprinted aimlessly into the vast forest and only stopped once he was confident that he was that he was alone. Adam looked around to ensure that there were no other creatures around before he would remove his drenched muzzled hands from over his mouth. Seeing that he was safe from the prying eyes of onlookers. Adam unclasped his hands and released a most sorrowful and painful outcry. He sounded off repeatedly crying out in loud bellowing weeps and wallowed mercilessly over his own tears.

Adam cried without restraint or reservation, letting his whimpers and cries fall on the ears of the traveling winds. It wasn't until the last tear had fallen that Adam began to feel well again. He appeared somewhat restored and rejuvenated by the experience, he attributed the acute condition to excessive buildup of negative emotions. To manage his feelings Adam adopted the practice of crying, which he flushed from his body like poison. Crying became Adams outlet and the process by which he coped in dealing with negative and unpleasant emotions. He began to adopt avoidance personality in uncomfortable settings and spaces. He garnered newly found appreciation for the utility and usefulness of crying viewing the intense cleansing process as a functioning part of his design as man. The bio-maintenance service routine afforded by mortal beings made man appear somewhat faulty and flawed. The treatment of expelling tears helped Adam to remove unsettling feelings and relieve emotional congestion. Crying provided soothing path of relief from the blockage and constipation of emotional turmoil foiling his mind and clogging up his thoughts. However, despite the many practical benefits obtained through the practice of crying, the act offered temporary relief and comfort from the weight of his troubles.

Adam avoided what he considered negative feelings which often-times provoked anguish and sadness within him. He began to ignore and suppress the gnawing feelings of discomfort focusing his attention on the wider range positive of emotions. Adam slowly began to learn how to better regulate and manage his emotions and feelings. At some point Adam was no longer willing to allow himself to become upset or irritated by the unrequited yearning for belonging which was at present unfulfilled. In his acceptance all that seemed monumental and important to Adam was now minimized. The unscalable mountain of trouble he carried now appeared rather trifle and insignificant. He exited the forest feeling amused and somewhat silly for allowing himself to become so bothered and upset by the matter. Adam intended to ask Tree regarding the whereabouts of his father later when he arrived home, but somehow forgot to ask after finding himself distracted and joyfully enthralled by boyish exuberances which seem to return instantly to Adam after finding the company of close neighbors and friends and joining them in play. Adam returned home that evening still unsettled and indecisive regarding subject of his father and decided last minute that it best not to bother or trouble Tree with such insignificant questions.

It seemed that Tree, had never spoken openly or directly to Adam about his father, and creator. Tree never mentioned a word to Adam about the prophecy or the fate of his destiny. She demanded that no one was to reveal or disclose these truths to Adam until deemed appropriate to reveal such sensitive information. She urged that the reservation, and privilege belonged solely to their king and master. Tree explained that it was only God, who could answer, and explain the overflow questions and inquiries that would be sure to follow. Tree knew that she would not be able to explain or provide the reasonable responses or answers to Adams line of questioning. Deep down Tree feared that a day would come, when Adams curiosity would draw forth the subject and discussion of his design and purpose. Tree believed reasonably that she would not need to reveal to Adam the threaded course of his path and journey. In all truthfulness Tree was uncertain as to the exact details of Adams assignment and frequently fantasized receiving an early retirement by way of intervention from the king. Gods successful return to Eden would serve as a day of celebration for Tree indicating the relief and surrender of her role and duty as Adams assigned guardian and caretaker.

Tree yearned for her freedom dreaming of the day she could return to the dull and simpler times. She reflected imagining a life of ease, tending to less demanding affairs such as managing the upkeep and maintenance of their botanical garden and home. As time went on, the idea of the king's tentative return began to appear less likely as the years dwindled. Decades had gone and passed since the kings last visit to Eden, his extended absence often led Tree to wonder if God, would indeed ever return for Adam as promised.

On the outside it could be assumed that Adam was content and even pleased to be living in the kingdom as a prominent and well know celebrity, however the truth was that he was not very happy. One warm night Adam found himself restless, and unable to sleep, he appeared troubled at the time plagued with unrest. He decided that a short walk and some fresh air would sooth his mind and ease his nerves. And as he carefully climbed down from the canopy of his home. He failed to take notice of Tree who was silently watching over him as he climbed down the limbs of her body before jumping down to the ground. "Where are you going Adam?" Tree inquired suddenly. The sound of her voice startled Adam who was surprised to find his guardian still awake in the ladened hours of the night. "I did not mean to awaken you Tree," apologized Adam offering a faint pardon for his intrusion. His somber voice appeared somewhat melancholy as Tree gathered from his tone.

Tree could sense that something was bothering Adam who seemed restless and disturbed on this night. "Do not be silly" answered Tree,

"I do not sleep, or at least I have not so since our introduction" she joked heartedly, but Adam, did not laugh but rather seemed troubled. "The question is why you aren't asleep, it is very late, and the moon is nearly completed its rounds. "I am sorry," replied Adam, "but I cannot sleep, for I am plagued with strange images whenever I lay down to sleep." Adam's tone seemed serious, and rather alarming. "Images" Tree repeated "what sort of images do you see?" she asked, with growing concern. "The images change from time to time," answered Adam, "but it's always the same kind of dream." Tree drew interest and asked to hear more details about Adams dreams. She encouraged him to expound further on his dreams and bare forth his troubles. "Speak to me openly," Tree encouraged, "tell me more about the images in your dreams."

"I dreamed that I saw the end of Eden." Adam hesitated to reveal, "I saw chaos and destruction enter our home." Adam attempted to explain his dream but discovered difficulty in recalling the intricate details of his dreams. "I saw Eden in a fiery blaze with all the creatures scattering frantically desperate to escape the impeding sense of doom and danger that lingered. The creatures ran to me filled with terror and confusion hysterical and upset yelling and pleading for me to save them. They cried out that it was my duty to save them all, and that only I could stop what was taking place. And I tried to save them Tree, I really did, but I could not." Adam grew flustered, and fatigued at the point of his telling, and dropped his heavy head and clenched his fist tightly. His hands shook nervously as he struggled to regain his composure.

"I tried," cried Adam, "I really tried to help them, but my efforts seemed useless. They ran to me from every direction, but I could not provide them any protection or guidance in which to help them escape the swelling danger." Adam sniffled repeatedly holding back a wad of sunken tears. Tree wanted to stop Adam from furthering his story seeing as he was growing uncomfortable with recounting the vivid telling's of his dream. She decided it was best not to stop him, but rather allow Adam to decide when to conclude his own tale.

"A fiery eruption filled the entire garden with a thick fog of smoke," Adam continued, "The entire garden was engulfed in a layer of smog and dark smoke, but I could still hear the creatures crying out for my aid and support, but I am helpless to act. Their calls and cries ended and suddenly I am met with complete silence. Thump, thump, thump, the sound of bodies began to drop falling hard against the floor. One by one, their bodies drop like heavy rocks against the hard ground." The eerie images of Adams story seem to unsettle Tree's nerves. She trembled nervously and was quite shaken by Adams strange premonition wondering as to the significance and meaning behind Adam's dream. The depictions of his dreams were intensely graphic, and much too vulgar for Tree to continue listening and as result going against her better judgment she begged and pleaded for Adam to end the story.

Adam stopped the telling of his tale promptly finding himself embarrassed by the watery tears that spewed and flushed his face. Tree did not fully comprehend Adam's dream but admitted that the dream seemed rather dark and frightening. Tree attempted to reassure Adam offering to pacify his racing mind by explaining to the young boy that his vision was but a simple dream, baseless and insignificant. Tree reassured Adam that on this night he did not have to return to bed, and instead encouraged him to go out for lengthy walk in hopes that the fresh air would help clear to his mind and relieve him of his worries. "If you do not wish walk or cannot find sleep tonight," offered Tree, "then I will stay awake with you, and if you happen to fall asleep, I will be here to keep away any bad dreams." Adam was rejoiced to hear her kind words and took a seat at the foot of her body. Adam postponed his walk choosing instead to keep the company of his nurturer and caregiver. The two stayed up together that night going into the early morning talking, laughing and growing closer.

This night would mark a monumental milestone in Adam and Tree's relationship. They were now beginning foster and build a bond and friendship that would later serve to stand the test of time. The circumstances of their relationship appeared perfectly enmeshed and began to reflect outwardly as transactionally beneficial to both parties. The earliest years of Adam's childhood were tender times where the two sowed seeds of love and compassion deep into their fertile hearts. Their love sustained and thrived and sustained over time coiled together like wild vines to form a protective barrier over their hearts. Tree no longer harbored feelings of contempt at her role and obligation to Adam. In return Adam affirmed an unyielding regard and admiration for Tree for assuming the role and fulfilling the position as his guardian and caretaker.

Tree managed to provide Adam the comfort of safety and assurance whenever in her presence. As a result, Adam began to open-up and confide in Tree jumping at every opportunity to share his thoughts or provide updates surrounding his strange dreams or whatever subject that surfaced his mind. Tree in return was beginning to enjoy listening to the eerie camp like tales that Adam produced, attempting to better understand and decipher the series of lucid dreams and visions. The mutual respect and admiration between Adam, and Tree strengthened their bond and soon enough Adam found himself, no longer confessing dreary nightmares, but rather began to report enjoying a peaceful night rest. Adam had moved on to explore a new subject and interest that was now beginning to surface in his thoughts. Adam was now comfortable speaking openly, to Tree regarding pressing concerns which he issued as matters of the heart. Adam disclosed his confusion over the subtle matter describing the sudden emergence of unfamiliar emotions. Adam attempted at best to describe the feelings, and desires growing deep within.

Tree often listened to Adam with earnest interest, while at other times, she merely, listened because her design did not grant her a means to escape. Tree, and Adam often talked open heartedly. Adam confided in Tree and shared with her his most private thoughts and secrets. Adam would soon reveal to Tree, what she considered to be her greatest fear, feeling somewhat embarrassed by his report.

"I have this feeling inside of me that makes me feel sad," Adam announced, "it doesn't hurt like pain, but it sometimes makes me cry. I do not understand exactly why, or what this feeling is or how I can I make it go away." Tree was attentively, listening to Adam, and could foresee the subject of his father was at hand. She felt a sense of urgency, as though she owed it to Adam to tell him about his father.

"The truth would surely put to rest all the insecurities brewing, inside the poor boy's heart." Tree wrestled with her conscious struggling internally to pin down her fears. But before the submission could take place, Adam produced a sigh followed by a heaving yawn that demonstrated his fatigue and overall exhaustion. Tree quickly accepted these lethargic symptoms as indications that Adam was tired. Adams yawning gave Tree the excuse that she needed to further delay the need to disclose to Adam the desired truth. Tree concluded that Adam was exhausted, and that the subject of his father would only help to prolong him from the rest that he so desperately needed. Tree promised herself that she would offer to resolve and answer all of Adams questions and inquiries whenever the next moment and opportunity availed itself.

It was now very late, nearing the early morning, Tree implored Adam to rest his eyes, and ultimately rest his mind. Their extended late-night talk had taken a toll on his youthful body, and before Tree could finish her sentence Adam was fast asleep. His began to produce the familiar noise that sounded from his nostrils indicating that Adam was no longer awake. The rhythm of snoring indicated to Tree that Adam had fallen asleep however she did not want to presume and wrongly and peered, up above her brows and gently called out to him, "Adam?" but in receiving no response she confirmed that Adam had indeed fallen asleep and proceeded to join him shortly in securing a peaceful night's rest.

13

The Hurt

The season of rebirth was steadily approaching. Nearly three seasons had passed since Adams last nightmare, and though Adam was grateful, he was now heavily burdened by the aftermath of insomnia and restlessness finding it difficult to sleep most nights. He grew accustomed to his new routine of exploration and would often venture off strolling freely through the peaceful garden at weary hours of the night. Adam walked aimlessly, through the quiet and empty garden in peaceful admiration of the silent jungle. He found the contrast of moonlight shone or rather illuminated much differently from the daylight. Adam enjoyed looking up and seeing the scattered backdrop of twinkling stars suspended beyond the bright glowing moon. The florescent night sky filled with glittering stars that stretched endlessly over the empty forest. The splendorous hue of the night was one that could only be observed those that were nocturnal; creatures and animals who inhabit the darkness. Adam being conditioned unlike other creatures homed the keen skill and ability to adapt and thrive in both the day, as well as night settings.

Adam became familiar with the various paths throughout the garden as well as the secret trails leading that lead to the outer regions of the garden. Adam wandered about his community nightly, in an uncoordinated and random direction unguided. The set boundaries and limitation of his wanderlust was a largely erected wall that stretched beyond the outskirts of Eden. Adam found himself oddly drawn to the mysterious object which the garden referred to as sacred grand wall. His trail would often end whenever coming in view of the grand wall peering off into distance. The grand wall was monumental structure that shouldered the very borders that secured Eden. The walls served as obstacle of great divide separating Eden keeping it safe from the outside world. Adams lengthy walks would often lead him into the pathway and direction of his interest and fascination with the large and mysterious wall. As time went on Adam natural sense of curiosity would draw him further away from the boundaries of Eden and closer into the trenches of the outskirt regions. Adam wandered nightly from a safe and distant view, marveling over the robust, and wondrous design of the grand wall.

Adam never dared to venture too close to the enormous structure that stretched far across the vast land like a giant lasso made entirely of granite stone and refined mortar. Adam could only gaze over with astonishment at the large structure that lengthened beyond a great deal and distance. "This wall is truly grand," admired Adam, "as it appears to go on forever." It was during these times that Adam would reflect on his younger years and recall the many forbiddances, and numerous warnings from Tree, prohibiting him from venturing near or close to the vicinity of the grand wall.

Adam recalled Tree's many warnings her words replaying over in the back of his mind. "Be careful not to travel too far," Tree urged, "and avoid the outskirts of the kingdom, always stay within the confines of the garden. The grand wall was erected, solely for purpose of keeping this paradise safe from the desolate and unfinished world outside of Eden. Promise me you will never go near it."

Adam remembered another instance, during a random conversation, in which the subject of the grand wall was brought into discussion. He recalled how strange the animals behaved at the mention of the grand wall, awkwardly, to say the most. They simmered their chattering to low whispers and offered nudging reminders regarding avoiding the topic and discussion of the wall with Adam present. The creatures behaved strangely and rather clumsily by abruptly changing the discussion and deploying other subjects and topics in its place. It went without saying that the grand wall was a controversially tabooed and unspoken topic. The very mention of the grand wall brought with it heightened feelings of tension and anxiety around the subject. Many of them did not comprehend fully as to why visiting of the grand wall was prohibited and discouraged, however no one dared to challenge the order or bring into question the royal decree. The very mention of the grand wall drew with it feelings of discomfort and awkwardness among the sanctioned creatures. In Adams presence the subject and conversations would often shift to a more appropriate and lighter discussions such as the weather, and news with each offering their observations for the day.

Many of the creatures, secretly believed that the land, beyond grand walls were desolate, just as Tree described, while other believed that beyond the walls existed a utopia, that would make their own paradise seem impoverished in comparison.

Often enough, creatures began to report hearing strange, and unusual sounds, echoing near the outskirts of the grand wall. The creatures brought their concerns to Tree with the hopes, she would be able to provide an explanation that would help to relieve their worries and quell their fears, "Do not be stirred, my good friends," Tree addressed the creatures, "we are safe here in the garden." offering reassurances to the overly anxious and panicky group, "I cannot verify as to the source of these strange reports, however rest assured and know that we are all safe, and protected here in Eden. No creature can enter or breach through our sacred borders, nor can anyone outside of God, penetrate the sacred barriers and defense of the grand wall."

Adam stood near Tree's side listening silently observing as the creatures piously ingested Tree's explanation. Adam heard numerous exploits concerning the source of the noises. The creatures offered a host of plausible speculations and presumptions that came openly from various accountings from those who had never dared to venture beyond the heart of the capital. A younger more obedient Adam would have regarded the cautionary tales without question avoiding any thought of voicing any reproach on the subject. But standing tall before Tree, and the other creatures of the kingdom was a naturally curious and rationally driven being. Adam unlike the other creatures would not be settled or pacified by fictitious tales.

"Why don't we go together" suggested Adam interrupting the heated debate, "and discover for ourselves the very source and origin of the strange noise". The creatures stopped and gazing silently on at Adam as if staring at something strange or someone unfamiliar. The group seemed rather annoyed by Adams brazen and prompt suggestion. Peering back and forth at each other, the consensus agreed that they had enough of Adam's arrogant, and overly confident attitude. Adam's bold outburst, and suggestion was not well received by the creatures as they shunned him away with blank stares and beaten brows. Adam felt alienated and strangely out of place amongst the group feeling as though he was a stranger somewhat unwelcome. He was now the center of attention, receiving cold stares, from a cluster of frowning faces. In an act of dismissal, the creatures brushed away Adams concerns and shooed him off. Ox who was rather annoyed by the intrusion and stomped his hoofs in defiance demonstrating his irritation, "Please man child," excused Ox, "can you not see that the adults are talking." "Yes," added the voice of another "we shall figure it out, you need not concern yourself with the custodial operations of the garden."

Adam was left emotionally bruised by their shallow remarks even more so that he was unable to speak out, or rebuttal their rude remarks with the appropriate response. Adam stood before the others in passive silence harboring feelings of insignificance. Adam became resentful and began to regret his decision to speak out or utter words to the unsavory group. The creatures continued their crass behavior by teasing Adam with ridicule and mockery. An outburst of laughter and sinister heckling erupted between the creatures as they teased and badgered Adam.

Adams inaction and silence would only serve as consent for further provocation from the creatures. If left unchecked these tiny pebble sized insults would eventually form into larger stones the likes of which the creatures contemptuous hurled at Adam. "Are you out of your wits?" yelled one creature "Is your mind so tiny that you cannot not understand? The grand wall is a forbidden area!"

Tree, tried desperately to settle the near erratic group, but discovered the sound of her voice was no match against the uproar of the small mob. The group continued their jabbing insults sharing unkind words, each comment meaner, and crueler than the last.

One could easily see that their verbal assaults were impactful as Adam face began to flush with anguish. A heavy weight of shame, and embarrassment fell over Adam as he listened to insults expressed by creatures that who he took to be his friends, and family. Adam feeling devastated and overcome by bitterness and resentment as his eyes began to swell with tears.

"You, have no sense, at all…" shouted Badger "no wonder your father has not came back for you" The cynical group quickly ceased their laughter and drew into a deafened silence after quickly recognizing that the insult had crossed beyond the bounds of playful banter into the realms of unsavory disrespect. The group turned their attention over to Badger and attempted to correct the arrogant creature for his insulant remark, however it was too late.

Adam was deeply affected by Badger's wounding remark, feeling as though a sharp object had been jabbed through his chest penetrating deep into his heart. The somber and melancholy emotions that Adam tucked away began to resurface and soon his eyes began to water and fill up with tears. The gates of his eyelids seem to falter and collapse beneath the weight of flooding tears. Adam finding it difficult to manage his emotions attempted to mask his feelings of contempt and disappointment towards his tormentors. A look of begrudging sadness began to form over Adam's face, and very soon he was visited by feelings of anguish and turmoil. An ocean of repressed emotions came flooding suddenly against the forefront of his thoughts and conscious. This realization caused Adam to give out a devastating outcry. Standing vulnerably before the creatures of the garden Adam began to weep and sob uncontrollably with a stream of tears pouring down the of his face. The tears seem to follow a similar path down the contours and curvature of his jawline.

Adam's behavior and strange display of emotions was unexpected, his reaction deemed baffling to the group of onlookers reacting dumbfounded and confused by Adams current state of distress. They never considered man as being a fragile creature that could be so easily provoked and upset by their meaningless and empty words. It became apparent to all that God's greatest creature was an emotionally driven and sensitive creature easily irritated and offended by belligerent and arrogant behavior.

A chuckle broke out suddenly from within the crowd that ended the long and awkward silence. Another creature mockingly giggled, and soon the contagious sound of laughter began to engulf the crowd. They laughed loudly amongst themselves and began to call out and make insensitive remarks in response to Adams behavior. "Look at the would-be prince crying like a pitiful child." "Yes," another creature added jeeringly, "maybe Tree, should tuck the child into bed as dusk is rapidly approaching." More laughter erupted from the rowdy creatures. Adam listened helplessly as they taunted and laughed at him. He imagined seeing their faces hovering over his head taunting him with laughter and ridicule.

Adam felt low and utterly defeated by the display of disrespect being shown before him. He was admittedly scorned by their apparent demonstration of mistreatment and ill humor. He took notice to the vast amount of effort, and energy the group exerted in attempting to belittle and berate him. The deplorable conduct and behavior of these adults was despairingly childish and immature to say the least. Adam was becoming intolerably impatient with the creatures and was growing rather compelled to yell back at the group and return equally harsh words foiled covertly as playful banter. Adam stepped forward before the group his face eyes no longer bathed with tears but was now stained with anguish and bitterness. "Silence!!!" Adam demanded, his firm voice and tone drew the intended reaction with all withdrawing into silence to his command.

"You have the nerves to laugh at my expense," cried out Adam, "when you all cower and quiver over the slightest noise." Adams words shocked and disrobed the creatures, "see, unlike you all, I do not fear strange noises, nor do I fear the darkness of the night. If none of you are brave enough to accompany me, then I, shall venture alone, and discover for myself the source of the strange noise. The very sound that seems to grip and frighten you all." With no further words Adam slowly spun around and began to walk away. Looks of panic and alarm began to stir amongst the faces of the group, now fearing the repercussion of their actions.

No creature wished to assume responsibility or ownership for Adam possibly incurring an injury or accidental fatalities. The fearful and somewhat remorseful crowd attempted franticly to renounce their harsh insults and pleaded regrettably offering Adam a host of apologies. They realized the extent to which the extent of their riddle had driven Adam to go off and charter the deep unknown. A few of the creatures took it upon themselves to follow behind Adam, hoping to somehow persuade and derail him from his motives. The creatures warned against the idea and encouraged Adam to reconsider his interest in venturing far out into the outskirts of the grand wall in search of the strange noise. Tree pleaded and raved loudly for Adam to stop and return, but Adam did not heed her call. He refused to let his burning determination be soothed and quelled by Tree's sensible and reasonable assurances. Adam was determined and would not be discouraged or detoured from his path. The creature that tagged along began to accept that their pleading, and begging would not persuade, or derail Adam from his determined path.

The few creatures who treaded behind soon gave up and stopped following Adam deciding it best to end their quest and let Adam continue his journey alone. The creatures urged Adam to reconsider offering him their final plea, but their efforts deemed futile and pointless as Adam continued unfazed by their calling. The creatures could only stand by and watch as Adam entered the uncharted regions of the jungle. His body began to slowly disappear with every step moving further into the bushy forest. The famished untamed jungle seemed to swallow Adam's body engulfing him entirely. It wasn't long before Adam was out of view his body vanished veiled behind a thicket of bushy of flowers and leaves. The creatures managing their feelings of guilt and remorse decided it best to return home to the garden. The group appeared sympathetically regretful for their part in helping to drive Adam away from the garden.

The defeated group walked back together in silence overwhelmed in deep thought and heavy consideration. The creature appeared concerned for the overall bulk of their contributions in upsetting Adam. They feared the backlash that awaited them for their undignified conduct. Their insolence and arrogance resulted in the consequential departure and possible loss and demise of the royal prince. The burden of guilt appeared to weigh heavily over the shoulders and minds of the somewhat mischievous group. They reluctantly traveled homeward stepping sluggishly moving somewhat unambitious in their retreat. They squabbled and quarreled amongst themselves, with each member declaring outright their refusal to accept responsibility for reporting their failed attempt to Tree.

To Be Continued…

Prince Otchere is a contemporary African author with deep spiritual and religious ties to the Christian apologetic faith. His eclectic style of writing and storytelling is uniquely tailored to Christ conscious readers, and those seeking spiritual wisdom, knowledge and understanding. Prince writes religiously with the intention of liberating audience and followers from post modern religious ideology that inhibit spiritual growth and development. Raised in a predominantly in the Christian faith, Prince draws his inspiration from the bible stories and now looks to add meaning and depth to classic biblical tales. Prince has professional experience in the field of behavioral mental health with masters level education in the field of Social Work. Prince is a visionary writer whose profound works offer conventional gems of wisdom as well as guidance to reader through his unique style of writing and storytelling. Prince draws his insight from a combination of spaces including his social, personal professional, and spiritual life. An author and a collector of human experiences, Prince possesses the keen skills of observation and empathy which he utilizes in his interpretation and retelling of famous historical events and stories. Prince is an existentialist writer whose works explores parallels between lived human experience and the doctrines which govern and guide human behavior. Prince writes candidly to his audience in a genuine an authentic narrative that help to highlight the integrity and truth of his message. Prince has an emphatically unique writing style that allows him to channel his mind and imagination beyond the boundaries of space and time.